CW00674120

Praise for Michael ....
&
SPY GAME

"Pass the popcorn!"
—*Amazon Editors' Pick*, Vanessa Cronin, Sr. Editor

"Brilliantly executed...First-class spy novels with a smart, gritty atmosphere."
—Charles Cumming, *New York Times & Sunday Times Best-selling Author of KENNEDY 35* and *BOX 88*

"A thinking man's thriller... A real adrenaline blast... I loved it!"
—Robert Redford

—"There's nobody quite like Beckner. Cerebral and unvarnished...with dialogue so sharp it's like dancing on hot coals. You'll swallow this book whole." - I.S. Berry, *Author of THE PEACOCK AND THE SPARROW, A New Yorker & NPR Best Book of the Year*

"Michael Frost Beckner serves up a judicious blend of showy action, political intrigue, ticking-clock suspense, and CIA one-upmanship for mainstream entertainment."
—*Variety*

"There is nothing like *The Aiken Trilogy*... Laced with absurdity & stylistically daring ... Beckner [is] a razzle-dazzle showman at the top of the thriller heap."
—Editor's Pick, *Publishers Weekly*

"Beckner is one of the most unabashedly duplicitous writers I've ever encountered ... Brilliant work."
—Stephen England, *Best-selling Author of the SHADOW WARRIOR Series*

"Michael Frost Beckner is the rarest of spy novelists, a beautiful and compelling writer who also has a mastery of tradecraft and a deep understanding of how espionage really works."
—Joe Weisberg, *former CIA Officer and EMMY Award-winning creator of The Americans*

ALSO BY MICHAEL FROST BECKNER

HITLER'S LOKI
Berlin Mesa

SPY GAME
The Aiken Trilogy
Muir's Gambit
Bishop's Endgame
Aiken in Check

KALEIDOSCOPE:
A SPY GAME SERIAL
4th of July

A NATION DIVIDED
Volume I: Episodes 101-104
Volume II: Episodes 105-108
Volume III: Episodes 109-112

Kaleidoscope

A Spy Game Serial

Part 1:

4th of July

Michael Frost Beckner

MONTROSE STATION PRESS

Las Vegas
2024

This is a work of fiction. Apart from the well-known actual people, events, and locales that figure in the narrative, all names, characters, places, and incidents are the product of the author's imagination or are used fictitiously, and any resemblance to actual persons, living or dead, businesses, companies, government agencies, events, or locales is entirely coincidental.

Copyright © 2024 by Michael Frost Beckner

All rights reserved.

Published in the United States Montrose Station Press LLC

LIBRARY OF CONGRESS CONTROL NUMBER: 202395118

ISBN 9798985729269 (paperback)
ISBN 9798985729252 (ebook)

Printed in the United States of America

No part of this publication may be reproduced, distributed, or transmitted in any form or by any means, including photocopying, recording, or other electronic or mechanical methods, without the prior written permission of the publisher, except as permitted by U.S. copyright law.

Jacket Design & Illustrations by Andrew Frost Beckner

FIRST EDITION 2024

For Michael Apted
who introduced me to Lynn

KALEIDOSCOPE:

4TH OF JULY

"When shall I be
dead and rid of the
wrong my father did?
How long, how long,
till spade and hearse
Puts to sleep my
mother's curse?"

—T. H. White, *The Once and Future King*

Prologue

*T*HERE ARE OTHER FAMILIES, *neither happy nor mind-fully sad; sanctioned to deception, these families kindle their lives with the flint of authorized deceit. Their pyre is "service," and it is "national security." Its flame is "duty." "Honor." And it is "faith." Thus fueled, these families allow this fire to consume their every honest emotion.*

Relentlessly.

Equally.

And to completion.

Without protest (which could only arise from feelings they never will allow), they slough the cinders of charred commitments and incinerated commissions, sifting them through iron-toothed grates to conceal their treacheries, hide their betrayals, and bury their secrets beneath a shroud of ash: fluffed gray, velvety, and altogether dead. With the whole of what they should repent girded and unobservable, they are unrepentant.

Unredeemed.

The Kingstons of Foxtail Farm are such a family.

For generations, Kingston children, amusing them-selves with summer-storm indoor hide-and-seek, in-variably discover they can duck beneath the common room mantel to vanish upright inside the Foxtail Farm fireplace. Still as fawns, ready-or-not, each in their turn is soot-giggly here-I-come caught. But summertime play fades for children of every generation. The "child" in "childhood" divides into "manhood" and "womanhood," and the wind changes direction, blowing "in from" instead of "out to" the Chesapeake.

It was on this wind—this first leafy breath of autumn, fireplace first banked—Lynn Kingston heard first its faint, its fluted moan. And how much clearer it has become, each passing year, that echo across the Foxtail Farm chimney top. God—

or is it the Devil?

—who mimics Lynn's own long-ago moistened lips blown across the rim of her first bottle of clambake beer—chipped-polish, teenage toes curled in sand and seashell muck.

This moan Lynn hears, Lynn shuns. Yet Lynn turns to it like a beacon. Like that senseless desire tugging inside the hearts of the barn swallows who return each year to the abandoned tobacco sheds—afield from the main manor—where the kestrels, merlin, the barn owls invariably devour all but a few of their hatchlings. This moan resembles nothing so much as—

Sometimes, in the instant before narcotic sleep drags her head beneath its alcoholic wave, Lynn relives this, and Lynn trembles—

—the muted sound of her mother's screams: "Ignite me!" Crying, "Fire! Redeem me!"

Thursday, July First

F INGERS IN SCISSOR RINGS.

Hands in surgical gloves.

Trapezoids and triangles fall onto a bedspread.

The oldest pair of modern household scissors dates to the 2nd century A.D. They originate from a Roman settlement on the Black Sea called, as it is now, Trabzon.

"The Trabzon Scissors." A tidbit of information. An incidental crumb fallen into a corner of Michael Kingston's mind as his brain consumed more substantial bytes of data relevant to running his Turkish agent, Orthodox priest Father Cevik. One year developing him. Another year waiting on his promises. Nine months and sixteen trips from Ankara servicing their Trabzon dead drop... to little result. Most often, Michael serviced boredom with online trivia instead of serving America Turkey's secrets.

It is a fiction that CIA case officers operating clandestinely in the field spend the bulk of their time a black silhouette with a gun facing down a capital city; in mufti pressing through sweaty, spice- and hookah-stinking souks, avoiding the fezzed fellows with mustaches curved to match their knives; sitting beneath Cinzano umbrellas, beneath fedoras, skulking behind newspapers at old-world cafes with demitasse cups, coffee black as the Italian sunglasses that hide such clever eyes. Hide hearts of devious intent. Of daring flash. The quiet American who speaks little. Who smiles not. Who, belt-knotted, flips a raincoat's collar to Nosferatu through nights of green-glowing tropic fog, footfalls echoing on damp canal stairs to long-tail boat breakaways. That mysterious, retreating, uncommunicative stranger who avoids social, transactional, and cultural interaction is a magnet for attention and, no sooner, the obsession of local and state authority.

The CIA officer—no matter the depth and the intricacy of his legend—is under watchful eyes the instant he arrives on station. From your first taste of local air, the local security assumes you are a case officer arrived in their country to make traitors of their countrymen. Even with a U.S. security partner and valued NATO ally like Turkey.

Especially Turkey. Slippery East and West straddlers that they are. Always have been. Likely to remain.

Of course, espionage is not something provable unless you and your agent are caught engaged in an act of illicit material contact. So, you play patient, but you don't play spy.

CIA teaches at the Farm that the best way for the clandestine officer not to get caught is not to go charging after recruits. Slow-walk your cover. Means feeding your embassy day job. Means keeping the Ambassador happy in the barn. A priority. After all, there's no extra nosebag for spies; the CIA undercover officer on station has taken a legit spot in the embassy stable. Taken a real job denied a State Department employee trained to do what the CIA officer is not. In the context of your embassy job—in Michael Kingston's case, Cultural Attache—you draw potential recruits into your professional loop; you naturally expand the ring of your foreign coterie to include nationals who may be or have access to (directly or through secondary relationships) potential recruitment targets. You edge them into that growing social circle where, with a little carrot to compromise and a stick to tap-tap their flanks, they come to hand. Snatch. It works.

It has always worked.

You hitch up valuable agents. Loyal agents. You don't get popped. And you don't get dropped.

Only problem?

While the Clandestine Service wants you to make your plays from the long-game book of patient/naturalistic contact persuasion, back at Langley, the Directorate of Intelligence (DI) wants every play to deliver a score. Deliver intel. Deliver product. Product-product-product. Any/all you can acquire. On this. That. On the other. Now. Oh, but did I mention by five minutes ago? By yesterday? The CIA DI: the biggest and baddest intel-devouring beast on the planet. Size: mistaken for power. Voracity: mistaken for cunning. Might: mistaken for right.

Ops officers who master the physics of counterbalancing the glacial dispassion of the field against the burning desires of headquarters look forward to bright futures.

Michael Kingston wasn't a "bright futures" kind of spy.

Michael Kingston did not have the forbearance required on the one hand and pushing him was pushing a balloon on a string with the other. And so, over two decades of postings to Asia Minor, Michael made his own set of rules on how he handled official cover, recruitment. How he handled product. He played all four sides—

Host/target country

Clandestine Service

State Department/embassy

Directorate of Intelligence

—against one another. Once he got going—got *them* going—once he forced everyone into a position of having no one left willing to monitor him, he stepped up his game and case-officered agents as he saw fit.

"A disruptor with his obnoxious cards and that ridiculous pen he's always clicking," Ankara Chief of Station (CoS) grumbled behind closed doors before opening them to "Welcome home!" Michael for a second tour. This, only after the Seventh Floor had welcomed a former Acting Director of Central Intelligence back into the Director's suite—congressionally confirmed—who'd snapped his Chiclet teeth, saying, "*That* Kingston exhibits too much of his father. Kick him back to whomever kicked him here. I want Michael Kingston far away from my Campus."

Pocketful of business card and a gunmetal Parker ballpoint. All Michael needed to bury his watchers in circumstantial contacts. The passing of more material than the opposing service could or wanted to handle, obligated as they were to report, backtrace, and write up his activities. Michael's cover could be tracked by the

Willard ("Please, call me Bill") *Bramson* ("Like the Virgin guy, but use an 'M'")—

Willard Bramson
Cultural Attache, United States Embassy, Türkiye

—business cards he'd glad-hand into waiters' and bartenders', cab drivers' and counter clerks' palms. Drop one into the "win-a-döner" rotisserie grill, free-lunch drawing bowl—every sandwich shop whose bells he tickled. Fed business card fishbowls all over town. Towns all over Turkey. Breast-pocketed/clutch-pursed random-jammed audience members of university lectures. Deans and students. Music teachers and concert musicians—violin, oboe, trumpet, and score cases galore. Art galleries, artists, critics—credentialed or champagne'd self-entitled—and a whole slew of "look at me" theater folk—directors, stage managers, actors and dancers—all the way to the theater-in-the-round that was the street: body-painted, golden robot mimes, jugglers, the magicians, once a sword-swallower, Romanis with trick goats, and always the pervasive accordion players who, as if by International Hurdy-Gurdy Union Rule, are prescribed to lurk outside train stations and inside pedestrian tunnels between subway platforms to make us all feel better before we go. Wherever we go. Electro-squeezeboxers who, by some magical osmosis everywhere and all at once, ditched *It's a Small World (After All)* and now lead with *Careless Whisper.* Because why wouldn't they?

A ubiquitous card for every last-damn one of them. *Click-click* the Parker. A note always on its back: *Cul-*

ture is YOU. America supports it. Call me. Pleased to meet. Happy to talk.

In between whirlwind rides on the cultural merry-go-round, Michael would in-and-out his small hours through the doors of pharmacies, doctor's offices, dentists, herbalists, athletic clubs. *Click-click.* He liked shoe stores—although he only owned three pairs and limited his travel to one. *Click-click.* He would open small bank accounts at greedy large banks. *Click-click.* He shopped three groceries: meats, vegetables, dry goods—four, when inclined to fish. Five, if you count the coffee roasters, and Michael did. Cellphone stores. Clothiers. Stationers. Dry cleaners and laundromats. Tobacconists and home goods emporiums. Libraries, bookstores, the late-night internet cafes. *Clickity-clickity-click: Culture is YOU. America supports it. Call me. Pleased to meet. Happy to talk.*

Michael papered the town until his outside-the-embassy time was more cataloged and cross-referenced, mapped, and reported by his watchers to their service and by himself to his: the Ambassador for his cover job (she wanted to poach Michael from the Agency: *"Mr. Bramson walks the walk. Fabulous attaché! So panache-y! I simply must have him."*); his CoS by writing meticulous (read: "wildly imagined") memoranda on all of them as potential leads for recruitment with their speculated (read: "non-existent") intelligence value—contact reports that would wend their way back to HQ to feed the DI beast chomping away at Langley until Michael gorged it to indigestion on his corn.

Foolish, maybe. Reckless, yep. Make-work—you have no idea. Mocking?

Culture is YOU. America supports it. Call me. Pleased to meet. Happy to talk.

Most definitely. And that part of it was not looked kindly upon. Mocking is the sort of thing that gets men and women dismissed. Not Michael Kingston—although he did more than enough to make it easy for them by taking it one step further.

Absolutely forbidden, not only by the CIA but every service everywhere, and one of Michael's favorite tactics: the "innocent" encounter with his surveillance. Right up in their grill. Michael would provoke this with a sudden doubling-back of path and purpose. If supremely lucky, he would physically collide with his surveillance and, hand-to-elbow, proceed to engage them in conversation. *Click-click.* Write his little note. Hand off his embassy card.

It was unseemly. It was using checker pieces on a chessboard. It was embarrassing. Required extensive reporting for both sides. Often questioning (for him), interrogation (for the opposition), or a seat at the flutter box, fingers velcro'd, chest corded. Could easily, and often did, sideline you for a week or three. Get you ticket-punched-pulled from station altogether.

Point of fact. Michael Kingston engaged in that little stunt so many times in Albania that the SHISH (Albanian State Intelligence Service) filed an official complaint with the U.S. Ambassador, who reported it to the CoS, who scolded Michael but found him unrepentant—or, as he phrased it, "Blasé—and too damn protected by that Kingston legacy." He reported to headquarters he'd squared away the ever-inexplicit Michael

Kingston promise it would never happen again. True. Until "oopsy-*culpa*" it happened again.

Culture is YOU. America supports it. Call me. Pleased to meet. Happy to talk.

Fancy footwork and legacy legwork. His legacy? Silas Kingston. Father. The retired, but shiver-and-chill-remembered, former Chief of Counterintelligence. Point of fact. The once and future most-feared man at headquarters.

So, it was *"Michael has a Kingston way of doing things,"* muttered at headquarters. Muttered at every station he posted. Muttered by friends. Colleagues. Muttered by rivals. By enemies. All sorts of mutterers and backed up/backstopped by two of those things the cat (read Silas, *meow*) let/dragged/kicked out of the bag any time Michael's utility was seriously questioned. The reminder of two foolish/reckless/mocking operations that would cement Michael's bona fides (mutter "field cred"/gnash teeth) to the Agency. Point of fact: a big F-U finger in all their faces.

1. The careless whispers of some break dancers outside the South Caucus Railway terminal in Yerevan—2009—and Michael averts a mass casualty event perpetrated by renegade officers of Armenia's National Security Service against their own people. Intended to provoke Armenian war with Azerbaijan.

A good one, sure, but go back. 2004. Better.

2. An unsanctioned bugging operation of Yasser Arafat. A beach casino in Varna, Bulgar-

ia. *Click-clack* chips, *clatter-clat-clat* roulette pill. For "to-see-if-I-could" kicks—by which Michael's agent got Arafat to brag about how he not only bit the hand but took some fingers of his former Soviet, now Russian Federation, sponsors. Led to the thallium sweetener in the PLO leader's coffee when—once again: an unsanctioned/forbidden, "What the hell's that guy thinking?" nifty trick—he'd (improperly) shared the audio with an opposite number at the Russian embassy, then (inappropriately) tipped off the Mossad to *that*. They went along and, best of enemies, rolled out an invisible red carpet for the Russian-red SVR RF hit team, who were able to get all the way inside the one place the Israelis couldn't: the teacup in the terrorist's fat, murderous fist.

In checkers, you make your peons kings, and you use them to attack.

BACK TO TRABZON. Back to the scissors. Well, almost. Back by way of this: with each encountered civilian, Michael made a point to extoll them with ad hoc/ad nauseum tales. Cultural cotton candy collected on his outings, explorations, his internet café clickbait misadventures. His Turkish, ranked Level 4 on the Interagency Language Roundtable, allowed him a fluency capable of boring the natives with "sophisticated and nuanced complexity." Business cards as strewn sawdust, Michael Kingston created an eminently traceable curlicue trail whittled from the out-and-about stomps and stumps of his elaborate afternoons, evening entertainments, and knockabout weekends where his dull conversation suggested an equal amount of sawdust between his ears. All of this because, as his father had taught him:

A spy can't slip in and out of a secret door if he hasn't erected a massive labyrinth of false walls to conceal it.

Not surprising, then, Michael rolled out the scissor story today. His reason? To buy time at a home goods emporium cashier counter to evaluate his agent. Scissors—which he could speak about for five minutes without using a thought—were the first distraction he saw, and he grabbed a pair.

"These Chinese scissors are exactly what I need. But did *you* know? The story of the first pair of scissors?" He hung a bit of silence on the gallows of a question mark.

The cashier leaned in. Blinked her eyes.

"Household scissors like these: opposing blades, center fulcrum screw—?" Did it to her again.

Blink-blink (nearsighted girl). Rope her in.

"First manufactured three blocks from here. The original pair of scissors. Invented in Trabzon." Pointed at her. "Your. City. China-be-damned."

The clerk snorted. Found Michael's story ridiculous, though enough a curiosity to push her glasses up her nose and share it—some sort of flirtation—with her manager. The older fellow frowned. Knew for a fact, nothing world-changing ever happened in Trabzon. Especially with scissors. *"Asla yapmadı. Asla olmaz."* Never did. Never will.

Through the grilled windows that backed the clerk and her unimaginative manager, Michael watched the inevitable: Father Cevik's flapping arms pinned like pigeon wings as the priest was snared at a *simit* vendor's cart half a block down the busy street.

Rewind. Forty minutes into Michael's two-hour Surveillance Detection Route. Run-up to servicing their dead drop in the forest hills above town. Four blocks back, seven minutes earlier. Cevik unexpectedly hurries alongside Michael. Performs a lightning contact. A photo envelope shoved into his case officer's windbreaker. A beauty piece of tradecraft. Better performed than Michael thought possible.

Indication Cevik believes himself burned.

Michael detects no immediate pursuit, let alone standoff/standby surveillance among the after-work rush hour crowd. He separates from the foot traffic.

Circles a set of blocks.

Enters the home goods store from its rear parking lot.

Grabs the Chinese scissors. Sets himself window-adjacent. In time to observe Cevik to the baker's cart. Cevik seized. Belief justified.

Aw, hell.

Turkish bagels flew; actual pigeons—wings kazooing—mobbed. Plainclothes security officers wrestled Father Cevik into their unmarked and waiting car. Gone.

That no one burst in on Michael suggested the brush pass had gone unobserved—

God, but it was a beauty hand-off.

—and Michael completed his purchase of the scissors as traceable cover for his fade-away SDR via the local museum, where he would bolster that cover and provide a choke point to narrow his pursuit if actual fleet-footed escape became necessary.

♛ ♛ ♛

THE PEN-CHEWING VOLUNTEER at the information desk knew nothing about the famous Trabzon scissors, but—

"Küratör yardımcımıza danışmaktan mutluluk duyarım efendim." I'm happy to consult our assistant curator, sir. He pointed the damp end of his pen at a brushy man, broad-shouldered and bunched. Called the man over.

The assistant curator resembled a boar. Serious of eye—which is the only way boars ever see the world—and dressed in a lab coat that had seen better cleaners. His rooting out the definitive answer to the proto-scissor question earned Michael a legit piece of time to refresh his situational profile. Confirm himself continued-clear of enemy eyes.

Kesinlikle! Most certainly! The curator was familiar with the Trabzon Scissors. The archetypic snips had indeed been unearthed in Trabzon. On the eve of World War II. Absconded with to New York City where they reside today, uncared for, unnoticed, and unidentified— *"çalınan mallar ve karşılıksız!"* —stolen property and unrequited! (that final word, one Turks pair not only with "love" but with "vengeance")—at the Metropolitan Museum of Art.

Curator suggestion: if Michael wants to visit a museum, *"Amerika'ya geri dön. Ve sana ait olmayan Türk hiçbir şeyi almamaya çalış!"* Go back to America. And don't take anything Turkish that doesn't belong to you!

With a parrying hand—like Moe slapping Larry—he swatted the air, gesticulating Michael to the street doors he'd arrived through. Michael ignored him. Out through the small main gallery. Out the rear door. Without pursuit. Without surveillance. SDR clean and out in the clear.

♛ ♛ ♛ ♛

FOURTEEN HOURS LATER, long-returned to his Trabzon hotel room—freedom still intact—Michael worked at destroying Father Cevik's photos to a point of satisfaction. A point of long-alluded, thus eluded, Kingston truth.

Michael has taken the entire night to discern their meaning. Now, rays from the morning sun construct themselves on dust mote air breezing through the open, lead-paned window—glass emblazoned white with the shimmer of Black Sea reflection—and this is what his agent has given everything for:

Twenty-three photographic prints. None of them from the same negative strip. None of them the same situation or timeline. None of them about anything specific or evident to the spy game at all.

Without communicating what these photographs would contain, they had, for seven months, excited Father Cevik. How he'd regaled Michael with child-like promises—oh, how he hop-footed and promised. Promised and hop-footed, and vowed he would soon acquire them. And boy-oh-boy: Photographic intel of utmost importance to regional peace. World peace. Glory on earth! He insisted they would be the crowning achievement of Michael's career. The crown jewels of international secrets. Old enemies exposed as joint conspirators; old friends exposed as raptor-clawed enemies. A secret map out of an end-time calamity. Though "why"—the these-that-him, or Michael-as-receiver—Cevik never did explain.

Michael's interest might have flagged were it not for the intensity of Cevik's siren-song. Cevik's passion. Cevik's God-as-my-witness faith. Cevik's civic duty. And what the hell? Michael was big-brother-fond of the collared, young cleric. Liked him a lot because true believers triggered that in Michael Kingston—an impulse to mystery long fathered out of him. Belief in, "Yeah, there are Holy Grails, and I'm gonna be the guy who spills one all over the tablecloth of the world."

Michael was a-okay with the holy man's *"Once you study the prints, you'll see answers to which I have no adequate words."*

Michael was a first-in-line sucker for true believers. Because what hadn't been Kingston'd out of Michael was a drop of hidden purity, simple and unspoken, named "hope."

One photograph after the other. Studied over. Over again. Michael had spent half the night. All he discerned were more questions. Lost of any connectivity. Lost of any specifics. Broader and broader. Lost of any determinable timeline/timetable. Any number of them obviously a decade, two—some practically four—decades in the past. Some, last month. Maybe yesterday morning;

no way to tell with the recent ones. Didn't matter because Michael couldn't fathom a relationship between any of the pictures and a contextual geopolitical event. Still, he committed to memory the unknown geography, unremarkable street signs, memorized unfamiliar building names, outdated license plates—noting numbers and nationalities—billboards, and bus stop ads—those he could read—and none of them meant a thing to any intelligence/espionage framework he could identify. Only one truth pushed through—

Turks grabbed my agent because they *wanted these photos. Knew he had them. Wanted him stopped before he got them... to me.*

It had been after midnight, after moonset and only when, prints put aside, time and place and specific content faded to background. And what had been background—a kind of static *Where's Waldo?* connectivity—assembled in his mind. In his memory. In his imagination.

Then he didn't want to look at them.

Instead, Michael searched his soul for excuses that career, family, life, loyalty, and the more-give-us-more, ravenous DI hellhounds had ingrained in him.

Authorized cowardice? After all, these aren't Agency-value intelligence. If anything, the opposite. Damn you, Father Cevik. There is no context for you *to know; no thread to connect these... To us.*

Aw, shit. Did Cevik recruit me?

Bury it. Not important. Not noteworthy... Not my problem.

Authorize cowardice.

But it *was* Michael's problem. Deadly. Padding after him, relentless, all his childhood, all his youth, all his adult life.

What washed over Michael Kingston with the morning's steady light—the most remarkable thing of it all—was that the course of human events once impacted by a pair of Classical Era household shears now met again in a pair of six-inch *Made in China*-stamped blades snicker-snacking in his hand less than fifty yards from where their iron forebear was forged, lost, found, and filched.

He nibbled on this idea to dispel the gnawing phantom of his mother; *her* impulse to mystery—

Doris. Tragic. Dead.

A memory no one knew he held, his mind trying to devour itself as soon as he understood the activity depicted in Cevik's photographs, the undecipherable "why" of their disconnected timelines and subject matter, pulled less gravity than the one individual, featured or background, disguised or plain of face, in focus or out, involved in, observing of, or randomly passing through the indistinguishable action: a singularity—a man as the Kingston ultimate no man's land—caught in each frame.

The Enchanted Forest.

Jousting knights on carousel horses.

A red balloon.

A man not my father who made my mother smile.

The telephone rang. It would be Lynn, his sister. A call arranged two days prior. Blown off eight hours earlier. Not because of the terrible news he needed to relay and the deserved concern it would cause the Seventh Floor once Lynn alerted senior management to Cevik's arrest, but because of the private course of action suddenly before him. The telephone rang.

A path he would inevitably take.

A change of compass Lynn would be—in all rights and duties, legal, personal, unspoken/enslaved—dead set against. And the telephone rang.

He answered her call. Reported the details of Father Cevik's capture. Did not reveal their brief encounter. Braced the phone to his head with the top of his shoulder. Bled off his sudden aggression stirred by the sound of her voice, frustration over things neither of them could ever say, and he transferred it into the cutting of the photographs to specific purpose. Michael prepared to argue. Knew he'd lose. Knew how to do that better than most. But Michael also knew: planned defeat was an excellent Kingston motivator.

"If you'd been with your agent, Turkish Military Intelligence would have captured you, too," Lynn snapped at his ear.

"Lookit. I know. I get that. And you're right. But I'm not right-or-wronging you here."

"Me?! Don't you dare—"

"The right and wrong at the center of this is Father Cevik."

"Give it up, Michael. Cevik's off the board, and 'a piece taken—"

"'And a piece taken is out of the game,'" he mocked her words, their father's words, as she finished them.

"Permanently," Lynn emphasized, crisp and clear from Langley office officialdom.

Trapezoids and triangles onto the bed.
Scattered.

Spread.

Separated.

The strange patterns of random falling bits of glass viewed through a prism of mirrors: inescapably bound symmetric.

He laid aside those fragments that contained the head and torso of his enemy.

"Then we're in agreement. Your path—your *duty*—is clear and unassailable. The only thing left for you is to get your lanky ass back to the embassy in Ankara—don't return to your apartment, don't chat up your street riffraff, don't stop for *anything*—because right now, this freaking second, they are forcing your identity out of Cevik and, full stop: You. Are. Blown."

"Three stops, and I'm not riding that bus. It's not gonna happen."

"Everyone breaks." The flatness in Lynn's voice indicated this wasn't a subject in need of debate.

"I'm not talking Cevik breaking. What's not happening is me coming in."

The photo scraps. The face of his enemy. An intensely handsome man of about seventy or so. Unremembered by Lynn. Recognizable only to Michael and only by his Russian codename, *Kalaydoskop.*

How had Cevik known? Dude's too young to know!

"His last communication indicated he has something big," Michael added with a hint of spite to stir her up.

"It's always 'big' with that cassocked fool."

Michael reassembled each Kalaydoskop figure away from the rest of the clippings—eight clear figures in all: different locations, different activities, different disguise, different emotions. Mini-jigsaw puzzles on a bed-spread.

"Precisely why I need him."

"Impossible."

"Anything can be possible. This whole region's a kaleidoscope. Shifting allegiances, corruption, terror, fundamentalism; you got money laundering, weapons, nationalism, oil, mining, tech transfer—"

"Father Cevik promised—what'd you say he called them? 'Earth-shattering' photographs?"

"He did."

"You ever see one?"

Michael shifted his jaw, side to side. Gave a practiced one-two spurt of air from each corner of his mouth to clear strands of hair falling to his eyes from his cen-ter-part hair. A habit of his since he first cultivated the California surfer shag. A boy ottering along the banks of the Patuxent.

"Less than three miles from Hollywood," he brags at college keggers.

"Hollywood Township, Maryland," Lynn laughs right back, crashing the parties to embarrass him.

"Nope. Haven't seen a'one."

His eight Kalaydoskops reconfigured, Michael divid-ed each figure and face into eight multi-piece quadrants. From each grouping, he removed a different quadrant and added those pieces to their own pile. Eight vast-ly different angles in a few dozen pieces that would make a single, octagonal face. A single man. A portrait unreadable by anything other than a human eye with imagination behind it to smooth the edges. Fill the gaps.

"He *was* gonna get 'em. Lazy, I guess. Never came through... Listen to me—" He retrieved a padded envelope from the bedside table— "This kaleidoscope needs controlling. Kingston hands on it."

"Enough with the kiddie toys."

Cadence persistent, words firm: "Lynn. I am going to get my agent. You are going to help me."

"Forget it! This isn't climbing over the neighbor's wall stealing oranges."

"You never climbed."

"Destroy anything you have linking you, our Agency, and our government to Cevik—"

"They'll execute him."

He dribbled the pieces of his Picasso'd Kalaydoskop into the envelope.

"He's a priest. He's prepared."

For confusion's sake and to torment her—a Michael quality as well—Michael added a handful of random background scraps to the envelope. Swept the rest into the plastic liner of the black faux-leather, metal-rimmed wastebasket.

"He has a family. We can save him. Don't ask permission—"

"Michael, we are not going there."

He stood. "Don't look in the mirror." Dipped into the pocket of his loose-fitting slacks. "Don't think it over. Do it."

His hand withdrew. Tight around a small object.

"*You* have a family! A wife! Three daughters!"

"Get me to him, Lynn. He deserves thanks."

A withering laugh. "Oh, God. Is that it? Poor baby. You didn't get to say, 'Thank you?'"

Michael opened his hand. Funny, the way random events pre-load future context. Centered on the dry, strong flexors of his palm: A robin's egg blue piece of sea glass he'd found yesterday. Smooth. Rounded. Opaque from beach friction.

"Second thought? Don't help. Might be simplest to let the Turks bust me."

He added the sea glass to the envelope. His expression showed satisfaction. Satisfaction beyond the object. Beyond the moment. Beyond redemption.

"Stop right there."

"I have diplomatic cover." He licked the envelope's flap. "They'll accuse me of espionage. Front-page my picture. Declare me persona non grata and throw me back to your sweet sisterly embrace."

"Fuck sweet. Get out of there. That's an order!"

Michael grinned. He addressed the envelope to Lynn. Care of a Virginia Post Office box. An obscure address with a zip code +4 suffix that triggered automatic retrieval and special delivery by the one individual who would do anything for Lynn. By any means necessary.

"Sorry. This conversation isn't between me and my control. It is between me and my sister. I'm betting my life she has my back. So, step up, sweetheart. Find your family dishonor; the whole thing's real now."

Michael disconnected the call. He took the wastebasket to the bathroom. Dumped its contents into the sink basin. Sparked a match. Touched one of the photo scraps. Flash. The specially treated photographic paper disintegrated. He washed the ashy residue into the drain.

Michael snatched his sports coat from the back of the single bedroom chair. He took the envelope. Took his leave of the unpleasant seaside room.

👑👑👑

ALL THAT REMAINS of Michael Kingston's two-day stay are the scissors abandoned on the bed.

Unlike the Trabzon scissors of antiquity, these weren't manufactured individually. There is nothing artistically or historically remarkable about this pair. They are one of a batch of one hundred and fifteen million identical scissors exported last year from China all over the world. And yet, adding symmetry, another pair from that batch would, in three days, be tucked inside an old woman's knitting bag. Falls Church, Virginia.

Randomness to become the deadly pertinent.

A fire-and-forget outside hire. Hers would be the scissors that would most impact Michael and Lynn Kingston. Their younger brother, Hal.

Not by the weight of history.

Not by a cut-out puzzle mystery.

By remarkable happenstance.

In two days, while America celebrated her birthday, those twin scissors would—steel blades poured molten from the same foundry ladle by told-to-be and thus-be-it-so happy lau baixing *forced labor—flick from the old woman's bag to cut Lynn Kingston's throat.*

To end her life.

Arthritic fingers in scissor rings.

Blood pouring; Lynn falling.

Michael rides a carousel unseated and paired by death to a red balloon from a Camelot merry-go-round stranger who made his mother smile.

2.

LYNN HAD LINGERED LATE at Headquarters awaiting Michael's post-dead drop call. Never came. Eight hours she'd spent playing "boo" with leering specters of worse-case scenarios until breaking protocol (not for the first time when it came to this brother), she ditched protocol altogether. Dialed Michael direct in Trabzon and was met with the worst-case, wildest-eyed bogeyman she'd never thought to consider. Couldn't believe her brother had gone so far as to summon it to life.

Let himself be captured? Over what?! A belated Valentine for his agent? Won't end with a magic arrow and a kiss. He's going to get his head Valentine'd right off. End up anything but sainted. Damn Michael and his insubordinate, sneering stupidity!

Two years given Michael to develop Cevik. The priest with the big promises. The unorthodox Orthodox who provided the barest minimum of intel to keep his payout going pocket to parish poor box. More than twenty times, Lynn questioned the benefit of carrying Cevik. Not only did the risk outweigh the gain, but time spent on a single weak agent was time unavailable for the potential discovery of yet unknown better sources. All Cevik offered was a *komboskini* promise of "earth shattering" photographs sworn on the knotted little prayer rope he'd used to tie big, dumb Michael's hands.

Michael: Lynn's hands.

She: the Seventh Floor's hands. And their shoelaces.

For the last seven months, if Cevik ever hinted, if Michael had even known, Michael never conveyed an inkling of what the photos would reveal or prove.

Her brother was an expert at "smoke-speak." Make hot, empty air appear to have substance. Every time Lynn moved to officially terminate the priest's service, the pair of them—Michael and Cevik—would produce enough petty-pretty intel to delight the unsleeping DI dragon and squeak past hard-fact, harder numbers evaluation.

All Cevik ever produced?

Once. Okay, three times (in two years): verifiable movement of jihadis through mosques converted from government-seized churches and abbeys used as stops on the ISIS ratlines from Iraq and Syria into Central and Western Europe. Rendition teams bonked 'em twice; last time, gave it to the Turks who backstab-secreted them out. And what else? Occasional oddments Michael knew gave the Soviet ghouls at the Russia House still cracking old KGB bones—forked tongues burrowing for marrow, even if it was dust—hope of an Evil Empire resurgence: Russian influence goals asserted via Iranian proxies. Crappy little tidbits provided to Cevik by communicants who were providing those services—culinary, medical, grooming, and social—like said "crap"—and still tended to Slavic praxis the incognito Russians couldn't live without.

A bunch of Michael Kingston "I grew up near Holly-wood" bullshit.

And Cevik's fingers kept spidering over the tight little *komboskini* knots, until here he was: out of prayers and out of time. The cord around her brother's neck.

Turn your life over to the Turkish MIT?

Forget the field day they'll have; that'll get you thrown in prison by us.

Certifiable Kingston insanity. Bats in the belfry.

And she would know—the old house had one. A belfry. More bats than Transyl-freaking-vania.

Always too many angles with Michael. But there had to be a legit one with this...or did there? People who talk about going too far. One day: they get there.

Never an ounce of willingness in Michael to model outcomes before he'd jump on the train— *"C'mon! I know where I'm going"*—and she'd grab his hand only to discover his train was a runaway racing a bullet with the insane idea of getting out in front of it and catching it with his teeth.

Truth. He'd gone far with the Agency; given enough rope, he's the guy who always... lassoed success. He did. Lots of times.

Please, dear God, let this be so.

But Lynn shuddered. Not this one. Not this time. This was a bullet Michael would catch with his head.

"Not this time," she spoke out loud to dispel the image of his death.

Michael would cool off. Sure. He'd call back. Sure. Michael always came to his senses. He was smart. Smart-ass but smartest of all of them. He'd slip her some lead, and she'd rein him back in. They counted on each other for that. And yet, as Lynn hung up the green secure phone on her desk, her gut told her, louder than any empty room utterance: *Sure.*

👑 👑 👑

DISSATISFIED WITH the government-standard white paint used for the rest of the Langley white interiors, Lynn's walls were painted with an Office of Technical Services copy of a Benjamin Moore *Pure White* sample she'd brought to them six years ago when the "whitest of whites" interior paint first came on the market. She needed it. Had to have it. Lynn never asked what the OTS added to or subtracted from the chemical pigment, binder, or solvent—it had to be something because they didn't use the retail slop—but once whitewashed, without picture frames or other wall adornments, and illuminated by a full array of recessed, 6000k bright white overhead lighting, her office was rendered shadowless. It made her feel the way her heart and soul never would.

For a desk, Lynn had rescued a battleship gray, utilitarian, pressed-metal monstrosity. Well, *she* hadn't rescued it. Russell Aiken—loved, lost, but always close by in living spirit—Russell/Rusty/*Him* had. Parting gift upon his retirement of two years and twenty-seven days (but who's counting) back?

The desk once belonged to Nathan Muir. Nathan Muir: The last of the Cold War dinosaurs. Murdered to save the lives of all whom he cherished and, collaterally, the rest of the world that came with. A hooray, seeya 'round, parting tip of the hat, dead. Aiken had saved the old spymaster's desk from destruction shortly after he'd saved the woman he'd chosen over Lynn from a similar fate. Back in 2003.

Eleven years. And seven months. And eight days.

But who's counting?

Rusty Aiken married her. Nina. They'd never had a child, but his adopted Russian daughter was growing up bright, funny, and compassionate, and they were all three of them happy—

But who's peeking?

And by that, all that had happened between Lynn and Rusty Aiken had ended up for the best.

Biggest decision I ever made.

Choose life. So, there.

The only personal touch Lynn kept at work was from her childhood. When she'd been happy. When she'd been delirious.

When angels could fly.

When nothing inside her—those parts that couldn't be physically touched—ached.

A tall, clear vase adorned the corner of her desk. Filled with a collection of sea glass. When feeling especially maudlin, Lynn would raise the window shade and let the sunlight hit the crystal cylinder. Let the sunlight fire a colored spray against the walls. Across her arms, her face, and her clothes. Then she'd remember what stupid felt like. Her real escape waited in the drawer beside her right knee. Otherwise, her room most resembled a psych ward.

I'm fine with it. I've only pulled the drawer twice today. Two times. But who's counting?

Headquarters-trapped, Lynn never had a chance, as her father would paraphrase OSS legend/Cold War sibyl Linda P. Morse, who, at her father's order, had Merlyn'd Lynn: *"To grab the lever that spins the globe; to give it a tug and turn the world to your command."*

Yet, for all of that/for all of them: Muir, "Aunt Linda," her father, Nina Alverez, Russell/Rusty—who'd remarked when he positioned the vase for her, *"I can't believe you've only had this to stare at all this time—"* post-telephone fight with Michael, Lynn didn't recognize the deep-past trigger her older brother's words already fingered. Not having witnessed what Michael was doing—not having its product yet in hand—memorialized on her desk all these years, practically at the end of her nose, right now screaming from her subconscious, willfully ignored/blacked-out/repressed, Lynn couldn't know that trigger was her father's lever, and Michael was handing it to her. She would pull it (she truly had no choice), and the world would spin in colored fire on a rage of light.

But, for now, she did not know.

She did not see.

She didn't count.

Lynn was a Kingston, brave and strong, and her ashed and buried secrets, where the answers lay, were the sum of all of that.

She loves you, Rusty. In a place inside her tender, growing heart.

Even if she doesn't know you.

Lynn opened her bottom desk drawer. The one by her knee. She grabbed a bottle of gin by its neck and levered a lot of it into a mug.

A moment's reflection; the weight of her existence.

A long drink.

Oh, it's real now, baby.

And the liquor burned its way to her stomach. Swaddled and quieted her gut. Put instinct—

Put memories—

Put her heart and the one true, swaddled thing she gave up and halfway gave away—

Into a stupor.

※ ※ ※

TWENTY-FIVE MILES along Turkish highway E97, high into the rocky forests of the Pontic Mountains above Trabzon, an unkindness of ravens soared among the mountain crags and crumbling Byzantine towers of the Vazelon Monastery. Through rubbled splits in the monastery floors—the ceilings above him—Michael watched them wheel across the sky. The birds reminded Michael of the carrion crow weathervane perched atop the guest house at his family home of Foxtail Farm. The iron crow with a bone in its beak to point out the wind. Michael stood in a shaft of sunlight, his back to a ruined fresco that Father Cevik once explained depicted the coming battle between God's angels and Satan's demons at the Final Judgment.

This was not that.

But something close if he weren't extremely lucky. Two minutes earlier, he'd heard the vehicles growl up the overgrown, broken road from the sea-bright valley. Heard the rough deployment of troops into the ruins.

There were more than one hundred hidey-holes, tunnels, collapsed rooms, cellars, treasure-hunter pits, and sepulcher caves for a fugitive to disappear inside. His searchers could take the rest of the day and still not find him if, even now, he chose to abandon—

This mission? Quest? Forlorn hope?

Boots kicked through heavy debris. Cascades of stone. The concrete-gravel crunch of the ruins around him. Boots drew near—Michael readied—boots receded.

Michael was bored with hiding. Just couldn't be obvious about revealing himself. That's the trick. The thin line between getting accidentally shot or looking like you're begging to make friends. The search spread farther and foolishly away. Even the ravens abandoned him to his lonely view. Although Michael didn't smoke—not even the occasional pipe like his father long ago that had made child Michael believe there was a contemplative, misty edge to the hard and terrible man—Michael lit a cigarette.

(Pack of cigarettes—second only to business cards in utility.)

He filled the chamber blue. Watched the smoke lift on the air—as though up the Foxtail Farm common room chimney flue—through the ceiling and out the floors above. Scent and smoke to draw his hunters ready-or-not-here-I-come to the hunt.

Didn't take long. Gun barrels leading, Turkish soldiers rushed the small, smoky chamber. Michael met them, hands raised. Unsmiling but without fear. They shouted Turkish. Same words shouted in every language when soldiers haul you off. Michael didn't bother to respond. They weren't looking for conversation.

Arms wrenched behind him; Michael was hurled forward. They didn't bother to protect his head, skull-thumping him through the ruined passage beyond. Like the faces of the frescoed saints scratched off by the hands of Muslim intolerance, the violent men scraped Michael's face along the walls of monastery hallways—once softly flowing with hymns and chants, but now little more than artless, abused and twisted, stone throats cold.

♛ ♛ ♛

SUNLIGHT CAUGHT THE BLOOD glistening on his cheeks as, with a boot sole to the small of his back, he was jettisoned into a small, overgrown courtyard. Michael tumbled. Lurched to his feet into the arms of a Turkish officer. Colonel Vural—an ogre by anyone's definition; hands, face, the skull beneath his features as gnarled as a disease-rotting burl—steadied the CIA officer by the shoulders. The better to throw Michael to the ground with maximum force. He kicked Michael, kicked Michael, kicked Michael—kicked him into the abyss of unconsciousness.

Before awareness escaped, Michael caught sight of a goatherd. His scrawny flock: dropping, bleating, neck-bells tinkling into the ruins. Michael's fading gaze: the untroubled boy's hands. Broken walnuts pulled from a paper bag. Grubby fingers picking the meat. Grubby fingers—morsels to mouth.

The goats munched weeds. Scampered. Shook furry heads, flopped ears. Bleated. The goatherd munched walnuts. Didn't care about the human activity. The soldiers didn't care about the goat boy. Noticed him without apprehension. The goat boy considered Michael without curiosity. The goats bleated. The goats munched. The goatherd spit a piece of shell. Michael faded out on a single word. Accidental to the purpose his mind clawed at, it came with his vision transformed. His own bleat of a shouted demand by his father. A living word and real, shelled from a quarter century gone.

"...run..." Michael choked and vanished from the present.

"Run!"

♕ ♕ ♕

Michael soars over golden, sun-tinged waters of the Patuxent. Up white sand bluffs. Across indulgently over-grown fields of a tobacco plantation built in 1693 and named Foxtail Farm.

"Run, Michael, RUN!"

By these words, his father's shout, he recognizes the summer of 1986. He glides past the moss-bearded, gray stone family chapel...

"For Pete's sake, boy! Turn on the juice!"

He flies over the emerald lawn, a tournament field between the North Vista Outhouse and the main planta-tion house, encircled by its wide porch, until his vision rides with the brand-new pigskin spiraling down to his fifteen-year-old self. Lynn, once more age ten and naïve

*as it should be, both inside and out, dogs his pattern. She
plays defense.*

❦ ❦ ❦

THEIR SKINS, BRONZED BY SUMMER'S KISS; their bodies
lean—limber willows that long for good, strong winds
to flutter and show their stuff. These were special children, their faces vibrant, open, exhilarant; their bare
feet churned in perfect sync to lift them airborne; they
leaped as one for the ball.

Interception, Lynn.

A laugh. A dodge. An off-and-away. Lynn ran the
football toward her father, the failed playmaker, Silas
Kingston. Edging out of his thirties and yet to his
prime, the emperor-curled, bronze-bust patriarch of
the Kingston family, Silas wore a *Central Intelligence
Agency* gym shirt—because if you got this far into his
world, you'd know him exactly for who and what he
was: a Cold Warrior as set in his beliefs as the American
bedrock set in the earth beneath his feet.

"Hold on. Pass interference!" Silas boomed.

Lynn jigged from his clutch. Ran into an end zone
marked by miniature American flags. Pennant sticks
poked into the grass. She did a victory dance. Her
race-car red hair bounced and shimmered to match her
exuberance.

Foxtail Farm's lady of the manor—luminous, tragic
Doris; she of the lips you only see once in your life and
look to kiss forever—sprang to her feet from the porch

steps. Threw her hands together with silly, sea-lion enthusiasm. "Way to go, Linny!"

Bent over, breathless, Lynn beamed at her svelte and gorgeous mother.

"I said, 'Hold on.' All a'ya! Pass interference."

"Dad, that was sure not!" Michael hollered with joyful laughter.

"No score here," Silas tromped upfield to Lynn.

"She didn't touch me. T-D Lynn!"

"Michael: she went up without looking for the ball."

Silas held out his hands for the pigskin. Eyes slitted. Demanding.

"Daddy?"

"Would I say so if it wasn't?"

Lynn looked past him to her older brother. She read frustration in Michael's eyes. Teenage disappointment eyes (because he cannot protect her and hates that she sees this). She looked to her mother. Doris could protect her (but wouldn't until too late), while her younger brother, Hal, having run up beside their mother, hopped, cockerel, and crowing.

"I wanna play! Somebody throw *me* the ball!"

Lynn jerked the ball away from her father. Held it, hanging it behind her shoulder. "I was looking at the ball."

"Dad! Can I play?!" said Hal.

"No tears, Lynn. We'll not have a scene on your mother's birthday."

There hadn't been, weren't going to be any tears before he said that. Lynn found herself blinking to hold them back.

A dart from a crossbow, Hal shot across the lawn. "Throw me, Lynn! Throw me!"

It meant everything to Lynn that her father believe her. Silas shook his head, dismissing the whole thing. Dismissing her. Calling over her head, "I toldja, Hal: this ball's too big for you! You'll get hurt!"

Lynn whirled. "Keep going, Hal! I gotcha!"

"Don't you do it, missy."

But Lynn did. She threw the ball. High. Arcing. Hard. Impossibly far. By now, Hal was focused on the line where the grass ended. The line of gravel where the driveway led from Foxtail Farm to the forbidding and outside world. Hal stopped. Hal turned.

The football, much bigger than his head, blocked the sun as it hummed in fast. Scared, Hal didn't flinch. Reaching, straining—

On the porch steps, Doris Kingston goes rigid, exposing fear not only for her youngest son but for something terrible yet to come.

—and the spinning football, dropping out of the sun, slammed *thud!* into Hal's stomach. Knocked him off his feet. Onto his back. Painfully curled him across the gravel.

For an instant, no one moved. Horror caught in Lynn's throat as she tasted the strange poison of her mother's dread. Their eyes briefly touched. Daughter/mother. Like fingertips; a courtly dance. A kind of living spark between them.

Silas spun Lynn. Flashed a hideous look.

Hal, making sure not to drop the ball, elbowed to his feet. The wind knocked out of him paled his cheeks. He smiled weakly.

Triumphant.

Doris and Michael whooped and cheered. They ran for Hal, and Lynn ran with them.

"I... told you guys... I play... football."

Doris wrapped them fiercely in mother-wolf arms. Her eyes met her husband's. "Look at my *lambs*! Just look at you!"

Behind them, Silas responded in his own way—and this was telling. Without Lynn seeing it, he clenched a fist in salute to her successful defiance.

Silas was a man who hated himself. Deeply and for many things. But he hated himself mostly because he loved his daughter most of all, to the lessening of the others, and himself the least of them, because he, like all wolves, no matter how much desired otherwise, can never be trusted not to eat lambs.

♛ ♛ ♛

RIB BONES on paper plates. Doris wore a crown of yellow tissue paper.

"Make a wish! Make a wish!"

Globs of barbecue sauce on sticky napkin balls, gnawed corn cobs—knocked-about skittles strewn across a white-washed picnic table.

"Make a wish!"

Doris glowed ecstatic in the flicker of birthday candles as her three children continued to chant. Their faces encircled her. The strawberry whipped cream cake.

"Make a wish!"

"Oh, you guys know all my wishes came true in you and your daddy."

Lynn observed her, soft-focused, through a piece of sea glass held to her eye. It cast the scene fuzzy. Submerged it in sapphire. She'd received this piece before dinner, given to her by Michael on the spit of riverbank sand below the old wooden stairs. Kingston sand. And as she took in the moment, Lynn decided she would add it to her timid (the idea was new) collection. She made it a rule that afternoon, glass would only be added when its color matched a flash of magic she could see in a moment but not yet identify: glass to memories, memories to save, savings to treasure until she could name their mysteries.

Magic.

(Like the voice in the wind.)

Lynn turned her tinted gaze to her father. He sat at the far end of the bench. Content with his Dunhill pipe. Behind the who-what-where question mark curlicue of English Mixture smoke, he watched Doris carefully. He did this, Lynn noticed, whenever her mother displayed outward signs that hinted at unencumbered joy. There was love in his eyes, and Lynn never would doubt Silas loved Doris truly in every moment of her short life. Deep and strong it was, and Lynn would later model the language of love displayed by both her mother and her father in her own adult life to never achieve, or possess, or to hold for very long anything true. She would, in those days tumbling at her from the years yet to come, hide her mind in a blanket of white, dispelling any color that might bleed into her soul from questioning why.

"I'll wish for you," said Doris.

"You *always* wish for us," groaned Hal in one of his silly voices.

Doris grinned at her youngest. He bull-snorted dramatically, wrinkling his nose to conceal his glee.

"To my Michael: for your loyalty." Doris blew out the first candle—Silas always put only three—and handed it to her eldest.

She pulled the second candle and bull-snorted Hal right back to blow it out. Pressed it into his open, sticky palm. "To Hal, my little one: for your uncommon fortitude."

All of seven, Hal didn't know what fortitude meant. He snuggled, sunburned close to her bosom, accepting he one day would.

Doris lifted Lynn's candle, still lit and flickering, with slender fingers. Lynn lowered the blue beach glass.

"Lynn: your faith in yourself must never know boundaries. Press it." Doris blew out the last candle. She gently folded it into Lynn's hand.

Silas poured a Sauterne. He passed it to his wife. "Boys, Lynn, your milk." He raised his glass. "To you, darling, who the Kingstons are blessed to call queen!"

The three children lifted their glasses—they'd done all this before—and joined with their father's voice: "Here-here! Here-here! HERE-HERE!"

♛ ♛ ♛

SIXTEEN SUMMERS LATER, *Hal stands clear-eyed and chiseled, wearing the uniform of a captain of the United States Marine Corps, 4th Recon. An unwavering per-*

sonification of fortitude; banner-bright and tall, he is a warrior now. Beside him, Michael is taller, at six feet, four inches. Though not so broad of chest or shoulder, he is unarguably the most handsome of all the Kingstons. He is without a hint of prettiness but carries all the charm of a small town you know is out there, wish your whole life for, but exists a town no one has ever found. While Lynn—who at twenty-seven only tastes milk now when it's in white Russians—Lynn, who has already lost the one man she might have stolen to love and whom her father's great rival Nathan Muir had promised would protect her from both her enemies and her worst inclinations—Lynn has her mother's lips and clear eyes and, like so many who despise one of their parents, carries that parent's inclinations and instincts at her core, a nuclear fire. As with Michael, Lynn wears a CIA lapel pin on her suit jacket, and all three grown Kingston offspring are shadowed in the cold, candle-smoky confines of the Foxtail Farm chapel.

Silas Kingston, edging into his sixties, his thinning curls ashen, stands with his children over a tomb opened in the Foxtail Farm chapel floor. He looks down upon Doris's coffin as he takes a bouquet of four foxtails and red river lilies from Michael. He lowers himself to one knee, kisses the bouquet, whispers... "Love and simplicity, you made worth having."

Silas releases stalks and blooms to the tomb.

3.

A PORTRAIT OF DORIS *Kingston hangs between the first and second floors of the Foxtail Farm Main House. High on the wall of the intermediate landing, it depicts Silas Kingston's wife wearing a beaded gown that appears a glittering crimson chainmail. The painting depicts her before aging. Before disease. Before death's brutal and disfiguring grip. She clutches red river lilies. She appears in a three-quarter stance, her bare back and turned shoulder reflected in a full-length upright mirror behind her. Commissioned and painted at the height of her passionate thirties, she looks ready to step forward. Hand off her vibrant flowers. To lift her feet and dance. To speak tender words in her partner's ear, their wit and provocation hinted by a glint of flame in her blue eyes, deep and clear and fearless.*

After Doris's passing, after her daughter fled in horror and self-loathing; after her sons moved out to marriage, to station; and after Silas began his relentless shutting down of the Foxtail Farm living spaces, moving day-to-day life onto the wide, enclosed, and comfortably furnished outer ring of the screened porch; after Silas allowed his vast collection of mirrors to dominate the corridors and communal rooms, he positioned the portrait of his wife at such an angle that it would reflect mirror-to-mirror upstairs and down into every space he forbade the living to occupy. And while there is no denying the Kingstons and Foxtail Farm have been haunted since three hundred years before her, Doris's image—ghostly as it appears throughout—is, for now, merely the reflection of her art, and she is unable to hear the continuous ringing of the analog telephone echoing from the kitchen on this night in summer, this night in July.

♛ ♛ ♛

PRACTICE MAKES PERFECT, but perfectly ghastly takes gin. If Lynn's bottle had been full when she'd first poured, she still would have finished it, and she would still have been undiminished to the extent anyone could tell she was intoxicated. Almost half a bottle poured—mug to mouth—since her telephone call with Michael, knowing after an hour he wouldn't be calling back, she waited to hear from the Chief of Station. Presumably, the ambassador would have been notified of an arrest. Or worse. But, four hours without word or alarm, she'd lifted the secure phone once more and dialed a number by calloused heart.

At the other end, the telephone rang. It rang again. And again, it rang-rang-rang—it didn't stop—and no one (that certain no one) answered her call. An old-fashioned unit on the receiving end, a system without voicemail or an answering machine, she let the ringing continue.

"Pick up... Okay. Now, pick up... Silas, pick up the damn phone!"

The wait of her existence.

👑👑👑

IN NORMAL TRAFFIC at normal speed, the drive from Langley to Foxtail Farm on the Patuxent River, east of Hollywood (but not *that* Hollywood), would take Lynn two hours. Already after 2 a.m., when she poured herself into her silver Porsche Boxster, whipped high and running with the power of its 390 horses, she covered the distance with thirty minutes to spare. Not once had she disconnected from her father's landline to kiss the large silver bangle, heavy on her left wrist, and drink the warming/deadening potion she could always feel, safety/safely sloshing within it. Until this moment, she hadn't expected Silas would answer—had been letting his bell bang solely to bother the old man—but as she arrived on the family's semi-private lane where the black iron gates loomed large in her headlights, Lynn realized if he didn't answer, she would have to see him.

👑👑👑

SLAMMING THROUGH the front door, an immediate left out of the entrance hall, and through the front parlor, Lynn rushed in darkness toward the sound of the telephone. She pushed into the kitchen hallway. The glow of her own ringing phone illuminated her passage in the vulturine antique mirrors, wall-perched in their kettle of shapes and sizes. Looking glass portraits for temporary occupancy that, once vacated, leave no history or recorded trace. She aimed for the light bleeding through the gap at the bottom of the kitchen's swinging door.

Lynn plunged into the bright room to find her father shirtless. In sweatpants. Two feet from the plastic wall-mounted, cobra-yellow push-button phone, watching it ring as one hypnotized. Upon turning sixty-five, Silas shaved what remained of his hair; dots of perspiration glowed on his skull. Silas clenched his fist. Closed, opened, closed. He offered his daughter no other acknowledgement than his secret, twisted pride.

"Dad. Hey! Phone's ringing."

Lynn disconnected the call on her cell. The wall phone went silent...until she hit REDIAL, and the loud little bell hammered the yellow phone back to life.

"You're drunk," said Silas.

"Least I'm not deaf. What's the purpose of a 'family emergency phone' if you won't answer it?"

"Give your middle child a rest. It's past four. I was asleep." He jerked his chin to the porch doors.

Since when's he sleeping out there?

Lynn peered through the French door glass. No sign of bedding in the sitting area. She hit the outside lights.

Good God.

Beyond the canted plantation shutters, the lights illuminated the back lawn. Boxes and bedroom furniture covered the grass.

"Your bed's outside, you nut."

"Can't expect Melody to move it all tomorrow."

"What? You're moving out?"

"Into the Outhouse."

"The *guest* house—and you're giving Melody our home?"

"*My* home. If I want Hal's wife and boys here while he's operational—"

Lynn lunged at the noisy phone. Smacked the receiver from its hook. It clattered to the floor.

"That's just fine. It's done its job. You're here." Silas smirked.

"Michael's gone, Dad! Picked up for espionage in Turkey."

"Naw. Turks don't take our people."

"Do when one of 'our people' goes to a compromised dead-drop—"

"Nonsense. Michael's not the family idiot."

"—instead of obeying the order I gave him to return."

"You *know*. When you start telling Michael what to do, he's going to do the exact opposite."

"Michael and I will never be the rivals you tried to make us."

"If they arrested him, they'd have reported it to our embassy."

"Well, this time: they didn't."

👑👑👑

THE TURKISH NATIONAL INTELLIGENCE ORGANIZATION, *known as the MİT (Millî İstihbarat Teşkilatı), maintains a complement of offices inside the Yomra İlçe Jandarma Komutanlığı military base on the Trabzon coastal highway east of the city. Within that suite is an interrogation center—four rooms for questioning, seven cells for that extra special touch.*

Naked and bloody at knees, elbows, back, head, and face, Michael is hurled into one of the latter.

4.

G WEN KINGSTON RELEASED A final length of hair from the hot iron to watch it bounce. Settle with the rest of her long, curly tresses. She dropped her texturizing spray bottle into her pink fishermen's net purse.

Damn little strings catch on everything—why these had to come back into fashion this summer? No idea.

She looked at herself in the mirror. Shook her hair. Watched one, then two non-compliant strands drop straight. With the ungodly humidity, her curls wouldn't last until lunch. Unless she kept at them. Spritz-spritz trips to the ladies' room throughout the day as if she were back in her early twenties, living on blow and blowing stockbrokers. But that was when her curls were natural, tight, and the envy of Cher's permed wigs.

Somewhere before thirty, the curls called it quits on Gwen. Maybe the white lines. Maybe the white wines. She'd stopped the one as soon as she'd met Michael, and while they say alcohol's a curl killer, Gwen diligently examined every label of every hair product. Didn't possess one with even a shot's worth of booze. As for drinking it? On average, Gwen didn't swallow enough alcohol to steal the life from her hair.

Just wine after work. I'm not Lynn—okay?

Liquor wasn't getting into her hair via her mouth. That's for sure. And an extra glass of wine at lunch isn't a gallon, either. It was just time.

Time on your hands. Time in a glass.
Time in your hands and down the hatch.

Age.

Being thirty-nine and praying it wouldn't start thinning with forty. On the plus: Lynn, who was a year younger than Gwen, already looked like her forties had walked right up and socked her in the nose. And yet, Lynn's auburn hair was as thick and as fast-growing as Patuxent River Basin kudzu. And fricking healthy. And naturally wavy like fucking river currents. You could drown in Lynn's hair. Or her booze.

Be nice. Sister-in-laws are sisters.

Gwen kiss-kissed in the mirror. "Love you, sis.'"

And really, she told herself, she did. Lynn had saved her and Michael. The first time it got this far. Lynn's mistake—a life problem—her surrender gave them the instant distraction/attraction/affection they needed; ten years of hope, and awe, and perfection. Melt-the-heart smiles; jingle bell laughter. Gwen blinked rapidly.

If you cry, you'll ruin your face.

She saw a gray and pulled it. And when the hell did taking care of her hair have to become gardening? Why even bother? Selma Hayek and Catherine Zeta-Jones rock it long and straight.

But those bitches' hair has body. Like Lynn's. Ugh.

Gwen's didn't. Anymore. Why she needed exactly thirty minutes each morning with the curling iron. The spritz bottle all day. She finished the last two strands and—thank God for small blessings—they held.

She adjusted her sports bra. Smiled at her reflection.

As a schoolgirl, Gwen hated her curls. Even though her hair was jet black and her curls were long, kids called her Frieda after the brunette-'fro'd *Peanuts* character until sixth grade, when her boobs came in. Then everyone gaped. Jealousy and lust. She readjusted her sports bra again for no other reason than to admire perfection.

Nothing "almost-forty" going on there, babe.

Winked at herself. Kiss-kiss the mirror.

Straightened the elastic line of her yoga pants.

Clipped her Cartier sporty tank watch around her wrist— "Shit."

Forty minutes in front of the mirror.

Late again.

For getting/forgetting the girls to school.

Whatever happened to regular summer school? Kids aren't required to go to that. *Never went, myself. And who the hell's ringing the doorbell?*

Like anyone married to a Company spouse running operations overseas, Gwen tore her eyes from the mirror; couldn't face herself, let alone what might be beyond her front door.

♛ ♛ ♛

LYNN: MORNING SOBER—meaning large Dunkin' Donuts coffee in her left hand, adding caffeinated heat to her alcohol-rich bloodstream. Allowing focus. Hand-eye/thought-tongue coordination on top of that emotion-freeing (or is it stifling?), ritual one-pop out the door. Enough coffee, and she'd carry all the way with what she had in her bangle flask before an actual first cocktail at five.

No desk. Not today.

Lynn would see from there what the night would need.

Or require.

She took her finger from the black doorbell hidden in ivy that plaited the white bricks of her brother's Herndon home like lizard scales. Like camo-netting over a gun pit. She waited.

"Rat rope—" what Silas calls Gwen's ivy. Nut.

Listened to her nieces talking inside rather than rehearsing in her head the words she'd brought to say.

"Why isn't one of you answering this?" Gwen's voice filtered through the door before she pulled it open.

A phony smile pleaded with Gwen's face to let it become genuine, then fell, unsurprised and inevitable, at the sight of her sister-in-law. That smile—in this business—is the one you're always going to drop. Hear it shatter on the floor.

"Linny?"

"Good morning, Gwen. I need to come inside. Please." Her formality and forcefulness passed the message exactly the way Lynn intended.

"What's happened to Michael?"

Before Lynn could reply, a private messenger approached from the curb. Lynn held out a hand. "Here, I can take that."

"*I'll* take it," Gwen said, stepping past.

Second-nature, Lynn tried to glimpse the label. Gwen turned it to her chest.

"C'mon in the kitchen." Given up. Dead-voiced. Gwen kicked through the smile pieces on the floor as she walked away.

There were other things Lynn could blame Gwen for—even despise her—but not this, not today. Lynn turned her cold heart to the warmth she could always draw from the smiling faces of Charlotte—Michael and Gwen's second daughter—and Leigh, the last of the three. The pair greeted her in chorus.

"Hi, Aunt Linny!" They grabbed school backpacks from vestibule pegs. Lunches from the farmhouse bench hunched below.

"What are you girls doing?" Lynn stopped, allowing Gwen to disappear into the kitchen. "It's July."

"Year-round school," said Charlotte with four-teen-year-old authority and a slight lisp caused by her braces.

"Summer school?"

"Year-round school!" Leigh laughed at her aunt, who brushed the soft back of her hand across Leigh's cheek. Leigh twisted her lips to catch Lynn's knuckle with a kiss. A little ritual they'd shared since... well, all ten years of Leigh's life. She'd done it—that wet little peck—the first time Lynn risked holding her as a newborn. Leigh was a magical kid.

"We're forty-five, fifteen," Charlotte explained.

"Okay. Good. Super then." Lynn smiled, uncompre-hending, letting herself look lost to the pair's amuse-ment.

"Girls! Head out to the car!" Gwen yelled from the kitchen.

Lynn joined Gwen. Noticed the courier envelope tucked behind the juicer. It faced backwards.

None of my business.

She waited for Gwen to speak, chance-out how far she'd need to go and how much she'd have to reveal in return.

"Tell me he's at least alive."

"It's nothing like that," Lynn hedged. "Michael's simply been detained in Turkey."

Gwen sucked a breath. "For espionage?"

Before Lynn could soft-pedal her answer, Gwen's eldest, Paige—the wow-pretty version of her father—wandered into the kitchen.

The women waited. Watched. Lynn stirred as Paige nonchalantly accomplished what she'd tried moments earlier. Lifted the envelope. Read the label.

"Not for you. Put it back." Gwen scolded.

Usefully deaf to her mother as only a seventeen-year-old girl can be, Paige studied the envelope carefully, tossing over her shoulder: "What're you doing here, Aunt Lynn?" And looking past her to Gwen: "You said I could drive this morning."

"Hon', get in the car."

"I-do-what-I-want," and proved it by opening the refrigerator. Leaned in.

"The car, Paige."

"What-ever."

Lynn watched her wander out with an apple.

"You let her go to school in pajamas?"

"Victoria's Secret Pink has her convinced they're sweatpants."

"Has you convinced. What are you two fighting about anyway?" Lynn took a charge of coffee.

Ain't gin.

"'Fighting?' This s'freakin' normal. You didn't answer me. It was espionage, wasn't it?"

Lynn gave her a knowing look. Added a you're-probably-right kind of a shrug. Said, "Our ambassador's taken it up with their government."

"They'll kick him out? Send him home?"

Lynn couldn't read her. Her tone was off.

Good way— "Send him home?" Bad way? How/why?

Glance: the courier Pak.

Too much last night, Lynn. Too much armoring for Silas. None of your business.

She laughed inside at the *I should just quit* voice in her head. "One good thing. He'll have to work headquarters a few years. You'll all be together again."

"When...? They admit they have him, right?"

"I'll put every bit of fight I have into rescuing Michael."

Fuck-slip.

"Michael isn't coming back, is he? A Turkish prison—? Jesus."

"He'll come home, Gwen."

You should *quit. Or hit the wrist; straighten out.*

Glance again: the Pak. And why did it come first thing/first priority/big URGENT stamp and Gwen not open it?

Gwen stared at her. Shouted past, "Is everyone in the car?!"

Gwen blinked at Lynn, as if this were all her fault—and maybe it was—more distraught by the second.

At least she's not blubbering. Crybaby-Gwen.

Gwen grabbed the envelope. Shoved it into her ugly fishing net handbag. Stepped for the doorway. Lynn blocked her path. Laid a controlling hand on Gwen's shoulder. "You can't speak of this to anyone."

"Who am I going to tell?!"

"Paige already asked why I was here. She'll ask again." Guided her to the front door.

In the entry hall vestibule, Gwen scanned the wall. The grocery bench. The floor. The mother's checklist for the forgotten—books, backpacks, house keys, lunch sacks. Husbands. Making her way to the car, "Paige figured out what you crazy Kingstons do the first time we were posted to Turkey—"

👑👑👑

MOM'S ACTING PISSED; she's holding tears. Shit. It's dad. Shit-fuck-fuck.

Paige didn't press the driving thing; she didn't want to risk plans brewing for tonight with an argument she wasn't going to win. She dutifully climbed into the front passenger seat. Looked away as her mother opened the driver's door and she pretended she didn't hear:

"—why do you think we wouldn't go back with him?"

Did she tell—? Does Aunt Lynn know?

I can't believe this is happening to our family. God, don't let mom do this. Please.

🤍🤍🤍

CHARLOTTE AND LEIGH bolted from Gwen's Volvo crossover and up the long flight of narrow stone stairs that zippered the wide, green grass slope of Pancras Hall Private Academy. Perched atop the rocky table its buildings had been hewn from one hundred and twenty-seven years before, it glowered gothic and gray. Were it not for the colorful banners and flags advertising the school's students, its award-winning STEM program, its championship football and fencing, its ever-solicited capital campaign, Pancras Hall would appear more garrison than academy. Gwen had hated it on sight, but all Kingston's found their education inside its keep; it was a link in the family chain Silas would never allow broken.

"It's about your divorce," said Paige.

"What?"

"Aunt Lynn coming over. That envelope. I Googled the law firm three months ago. '*Family* Law'? What a pathetic joke."

Between Lynn's visit and now this, Gwen could only gape. The passing bell rang over the loudspeaker. "You don't know what you're talking about. Go."

"You think I haven't heard you and Daddy on the phone?!"

Gwen smelled her daughter's sweet apple breath hot in her face. Paige slammed the door. Had Gwen heard a muttered "bitch"? Flaunting the demerit, Paige beat feet up the grassy hillside. Gwen swallowed, but the lump she'd been fighting since Lynn, refused to go away. She hated her tears.

Puffy eyes look terrible for clients.

Paige reached the sidewalk ringing the exterior walls and stopped.

Turn around. She'll turn around. Please, turn around?

Paige waited on a classmate. From the upper parking lot. A boy. Gwen didn't know him.

Needs a haircut. And what's with the Harlequin shoes?

Gwen cringed as Paige thrust her hand into the impertinent Romeo's—

Degenerate smirked at me!

—back pocket. Paige squeezed his ass cheek for her mother. The two walked beneath the heavy stone arch of the main gates and disappeared into the student mob filing into the quad. It was summer, and one-and-all, the students wished for pitchforks.

♛ ♛ ♛

MICHAEL. NAKED—that hadn't changed. Handcuffed to a chair. He faced Colonel Vural, who held an open American diplomatic passport six inches from his purpled, bloodied, swollen face.

"So, you admit this is false?"

"You deaf or stupid? I've admitted fifty times: I'm CIA."

Michael's direct and obvious honesty ran counter to everything the Turkish colonel knew. Or understood. Made him twitchy.

"If you assume we won't prosecute you, even execute you, because you're American—"

"What I know is this: if you don't release me and Father Cevik to the U.S. Embassy—"

"The priest, then, is your agent?"

"Within a week you'll have lost your country's most important security partner and strongest ally. With no spare parts from Uncle Sam, your F-16s will be falling out of the sky. Half your military will be non-functioning—"

"This isn't working." Colonel Vural hefted his chair. With it, the ogre beat Michael to the floor.

👑 👑 👑

MELODY KINGSTON HAD NEVER owned a new car, much less received one as a birthday present. In twenty-eight years, she'd only had these last seven birthdays any good at all. And, in fact, this wasn't a "car" at all, but the biggest, candy-apple-ist, bad-assed, good-bye mama, *white*-girl pickup truck she'd ever seen—let alone clambered inside. Hell, let alone grip the wheel.

Memory hit:

Oscar Meyers blister on a coat hanger. Sleeve of Pringles. Jug of root beer. Dolley Madison Chocolate Zinger.

Awakened by drizzle. By Mississippi Mud (faint turpentine) snores. By embers sizzling in the fire—

Relief: the pistol that made her birthday nightmare possible still has all its bullets.

The real "goodbye Mama"; happy big-girl eleven to me.

Oh, this great, bellowing truck. It wonderstruck Melody as much as if Hal had presented her with a rhinoceros and handed her a saddle. And none of that diminished the magnitude of her joy at the knowledge she was loved and worthy such an exorbitant gift from a husband who had secretly saved for it by shaving off slivers of combat and hazardous duty pay while he was absent; by faking extra base duty to moonlight security at a construction site; then, because he wanted some added performance upgrades, sold all but one of his hunting rifles and all of his bird guns. And he'd kept the whole thing secret.

A birthday secret: *her* husband.

Strong, brave, patriot, selfless: Hal. My everything.

Because he believed *this* truck was the perfect combination of sexy and safety to both show off his wife and protect his family during sudden and secret deployments. It had only held Melody's terror a week before she fell in love with—as the twins dubbed it— "Billy Goats Gruff."

Melody grinned ear-to-ear as she slew onto the lane. Hit the gate remote. Waited in the rumbling, grumbling Ram 1500 before she drove through the gates of Foxtail Farm where all things measured small and transitory against the legendary and shameful plantation.

The twins, Jack and Little Silas, descended like seven-year-old paratroopers from the crew cab. Shouts of "Grampa! Grampa!" equal to the *"Geronimo!"* tradition of the Army Airborne School back at Fort Benning, Georgia. Where their daddy had gotten his jump wings on training assignment from Bravo Company, 4th Reconnaissance Battalion, Smyrna.

Smyrna: the Naval Base where they had been born. Off-base: the bar where she'd first set sight on Hal.

They ran toward the figure of Silas Kingston, sitting in the center of the overgrown back lawn amidst boxes of clothing and possessions. All of it was damp from a random shower that had raced in from the bay on the morning breeze, only to be hurried off by the fiery sun that beat to stillness the ghostly property.

Birds sang, insects thrummed with wings and fiddle-feet, and Silas stared at his open hands barely reacting to the boys gamboling his way. He lifted his face as they butted into him.

"Your head'll burn sitting there." Melody hoped to catch his eye.

Silas roused himself. Drew each boy into the easy circle of an arm. He offered Melody a sly smile to meet her reproach/approach. "My favorite daughter."

"My favorite father-in-law." She met him with a hug. A kiss on the cheek.

He shut his eyes for a moment, absorbing her affection and the natural brightness Melody exuded everywhere with everyone. Melody Kingston blazed with the dazzle of a sunny day after a week of snow.

He took her hand and told her truthfully, "I'm happy you accepted this invitation."

The back of her hand shone warmly, its skin the color of the tobacco that once flourished here, harvested by people connected to the half of her bloodline who came to America on wooden ships in black iron chains.

Silas focused on the boys. "And you brought my little 'goons with you!"

"We're not goons," they cried. "We're your dray-goons!" They exchanged this ritual greeting, Silas had taught them, and the old man chuckled.

Melody's smile matched her sons', and she, like them, believed they were talking about dragons rather than a rank of soldiers useful for wasting at Waterloos.

"I said I'd help with the heavy stuff. I'm hoping it's still inside the main house."

"It isn't. I did not want to weigh you down."

Melody shook her head in a mock-scolding manner, loving eyes communicating he could share the thing—whatever it was—that weighed upon his spirit. If he wanted. Silas appeared to know this. He relaxed into that knowledge. Relaxed into Melody's welcome presence.

He trooped to the North Vista Outhouse's front steps. Silas grabbed a worn football. "You're taking the rest of it *and* putting it all away. I want my new billet shipshape when I report. Right now, me-'n'-my dragoons got us some football to do."

He met their eager eyes and tossed the ball in small spirals alongside his bullet-headed skull.

5.

THE CLAVICLE BRIEFING BOOK Lynn distributed to the hastily assembled action team who filed into Deputy Director for Operations Gary Gravin's private conference room, was classified and cover-stamped TOP SECRET. This was unusual. SKELETON KEY, the operation CLAVICLE nested within, had—until 7 a.m. this morning—been classified one level below, at SE-CRET.

The difference in the matter hinged on the "damage to national security" the compromise of said operation would cause; at issue was the changing of SECRET's single attributive adjective "serious" into the intensifier plus stronger attributive "exceptionally grave" of TOP SECRET. SKELETON KEY was the record and analysis of her brother Michael's two years case officering Father Cevik out of Ankara Station. And, while running a foreign agent behind the back of a NATO ally, if exposed, might prove to be a proposition "exceptionally grave" (like being buried in one) for the agent, in the grand scheme of things, Cevik's exposure was more of an embarrassment to the CIA than anything else. Before Michael's outrageous stunt, the loss of Cevik—although tragic for the priest—would have caused little more than Turkish indignance and U.S. intransigent, blatantly feigned ignorance.

CLAVICLE, on the other hand—bad news. Worse business. The loss of a CIA officer actively engaged in on-the-ground espionage against a NATO ally—that undoubtedly would cause "exceptionally grave" damage. Not from secrets revealed, but in an across-the-international-board downgrade of trust and reciprocity wherever American presence was *overtly* expressed. Meaning American allies, or any foreign power America courted or was already in bed with, would distrust the Agency—more than they already did—for years to come.

The unspoken truth: everyone fooled around behind the backs of their partners; the acknowledged rule to that is you damn sure don't get caught with your pants down doing it.

Lynn's briefing was unflinching. If SKELETON KEY became manifest through CLAVICLE—meaning through the exposure of Michael Kingston discovered *in flagrante delicto*—the blowback to CIA operations across the globe would be large. Would be troublesome. It was a shit hitting the fan moment, and Michael had stepped in the pile. In Lynn's deeper imagined context, her write-up was an act of rotating the fan and aiming it at the room. She saw its result in the faces of her colleagues reading-in.

Around DDO Gravin's mahogany table, their grimaces, their flinching revulsion as the fan blades of her report cut from shit to shoe to foot, chop, chop, chopping Michael from toenail to surfer-mop top, the men and women of the action team raced one another to the end, looking for the best way to wash/rinse/repeat Michael's bloody remains from their shirtfronts and out of sight.

Lynn made eye contact with everyone in the room before she spoke. "Official response out of Ankara is no contact between Michael Kingston and Turkish authorities. But page seven... A lookout at the dead drop confirms Michael *did* return and *was* taken by elements of the Turkish National Intelligence Organization."

She emphasized this, thumbing the remote to the appropriate slide on the PowerPoint version of CLAVICLE displayed on the monitor behind her. A cellphone photo of the goatherd's walnut sack. A sketch by grubby fingers. The shoulder insignia worn by Colonel Vural and his troops at Michael's capture.

"I'm confused," said the first analyst. "Your brother loses an agent en route to a dead drop. You order him back to the embassy. Yet he *proceeds* to the compromised dead drop?" The first analyst let her question ripen in the silence.

Morton Drexler—Associate Deputy Director, Counterintelligence—foxed the low-hanging fruit. "Risk versus gain: there must have been something valuable at the drop for Michael to risk going. Maybe those photos Michael's been promising from Father Cevik?" He riffled the pages of his book to accentuate their absence.

A large "Remember the Alamo" Texan of fifty with large and secret appetites—straight from the Farm, Silas Kingston had made Morton Drexler his protégé. Tutored him in ruthlessness. Morton Drexler had achieved everything Silas desired for him; it had been Drexler who ran the soft coup against Silas's many years-long second-in-command, Meryl Hofmeyr—

"She knows too many secrets, Morton. Shows too little loyalty to leave her in charge and with clearance when I retire," Silas whispered in his ear.

Drexler drove Silas's knife in Meryl Hofmeyr's back, believing he'd learned his last lesson. Only when Silas left did Drexler understand he'd missed the extra credit at the bottom of the final exam.

"Director, it would be prudent if, when I go, you replace me outside my circle. What with the Hofmeyr affair? Counterintelligence needs a fresh and unsullied set of hands on the tiller. Agreed?"

Silas Kingston gone? Hallelujah. Anything— "Have at it."

Now an adjunct to the political appointee Silas maneuvered to the top of the division, Drexler ran things day-to-day in his department, but without fiat. Operated with the kind of hollow ache as when the blade is pulled out of *your* back and the can't-reach hole is left to fester and to rot.

"Michael gave you no indication he was going to the compromised location?" said DDO Gravin.

Lynn appreciated his deflection. "None whatsoever, Gary."

He'd always had her back since he took her under his wing and created her unique position as Staff Operations officer East Asia on Permanent Assignment, Office of Deputy Director Operations, National Clandestine Service.

Drexler ignored the exchange. Scoffed: "Turks rolled Father Cevik eighteen hours before you spoke with

Michael; they'd have swept the drop clean before Michael went back. He'd have no reason to return—*except* to be taken."

"Good, Drexler," said Lynn. "To ensure his agent gets killed and he's tortured and exposed as an American spy? Silas always said you were a genius."

Lynn could pinpoint the moment her instinctive dislike for the man turned to active loathing. It went back to the days after TIME MACHINE. A TOP SECRET SIGINT operation out of Havana she'd wrested from her father a dozen years ago—saw to it Silas Kingston and his Counterintelligence minions never made the bigot list. Drexler, on his own puerile initiative (meaning under Silas orders), had attempted to destroy Russell Aiken, who'd run the Cuban op, over the on-mission death of OTS officer Amy Kim. She'd beaten Drexler/i.e., Daddy, on that one too.

One of Langley's most highly protected secrets, even the DDO was restricted from TIME MACHINE, its tragedies, and its wild success. With Silas gone, it was part of the reason DDO Gravin kept her close.

"But they haven't exposed him," said Drexler. "Have they?"

"You saying my brother's turned, you sonuvabitch?"

"Easy, Lynn," said the DDO.

Drexler spread his hands and gave a malicious grin. "Lynn, you got me all wrong. I was working for your daddy before any a'you three whip-snaps ever got here. I'm family too."

Lynn looked askance. Morton Drexler wasn't family, and from there, his cancer grew.

"'Turned,'" he drawled, "is a two-ladle a'gravy word. I'm still waitin' on the biscuit."

She hated his stupid sayings, which is precisely why he used them. "Look, regardless of the reason he went back, my brother did. He *was* captured."

"For those of us in Counterintelligence, the reason is the hound's tooth on our ankle. The reason is most important."

"No. Michael's safety is most important, which—page twenty—" she clicked her remote, "I have a proposal for securing."

👑 👑 👑

A BUCKET OF WATER sluiced across Michael. Curled on the floor, drifting in and out of consciousness since his beating, the wet and the cold shocked him awake. Impetus to stumble to his feet. Scuttle backward. The two guards he'd had since capture braced him. One ready with retractable steel baton. The other spun him. Manacled his wrists. They shoveled him from his cell. Down a flight of stone stairs to a basement where the bullet-pocked concrete wall they shoved him against, stood testament to what happened here.

Michael rolled, chest to shoulders; he braced his back against the rough surface. He faced the brutish colonel who measured Michael's level of consciousness. Animal eyes finding satisfaction that Michael was clearheaded enough to know exactly where he stood and what was about to happen, Colonel Vural nodded to a waiting lieutenant.

The lieutenant cracked a break-open revolver. Loaded one bullet into the firing chamber. Snapped the pistol closed.

The bullet wasn't for Michael, but for the Turkish Orthodox Priest, Michael's agent, Father Cevik, blood-crusty from his own interrogation, head lolling, slumped in a chair in the room's darkest corner.

"Father!" Michael lunged.

Slammed back into the wall. His shoulder— Baton-crunch. Hard.

Father Cevik lifted his head. Squinched his face. Squinted through swollen eyelids. "Michael...?"

"Kalaydoskop!"

Cevik: "*Whee*—The *whee*... Wheel. Again. Turns."

"*Both* wheels?"

Michael's guard plunged the butt end of his baton into Michael's stomach. Michael doubled over. Spewed bile.

The Turkish colonel snarled in his throat. What with all the work he'd put into these two, their first exchange of words was something he'd not heard a whisper of from either. *"Onunla olsun!"* Get on with it!

The lieutenant aimed his pistol at Father Cevik and pulled the trigger.

Click. The weapon misfired.

Father Cevik strained toward Michael. Croaked out: "Your father— The— G-L-A—"

Vural pulled his sidearm—

"—T-I-S—"

—and finished the job—*BANG!* —right.

The lieutenant shoved his ineffective revolver into its holster. Dragged Cevik from his chair. A light flickered in Father Cevik's eyes— "He's not. Blood..." —and he was dead.

Colonel Vural stepped over his corpse. He tapped Michael's bruised cheek with the barrel of the execution gun. Spoke as if bestowing a favor. "I hope you like to dig."

"Bury him yourself."

"We incinerate trash. The digging is for your grave."

♛ ♛ ♛

CHARLOTTE AND LEIGH separated from the rush of St. Pancras students anxious to get to a summer day already half-denied. The girls buckled into the backseat as their mother said, "Where's Paige?"

The girls played dumb. Gwen's cellphone rang.

"Hello?"

"Mom, it's me," Paige spoke, plaintive to her ear.

"We're waiting, hun."

"I'm with Morgan."

♛ ♛ ♛

AND INDEED, SHE WAS, saying this with a wink to her best friend Morgan Eiger, a refined beauty of eighteen. An enchantress with a crazy streak.

"Are you angry with me?" Paige spoke into her device, speaker *ON* for Morgan to hear.

"Paige..." came her mother's exasperated response.

"'Cause I feel terrible. I love you. And I love Dad. I love our family."

"I do, too. Where are you?"

"I'm sorry how I behaved."

"It's okay. Where are you— What are you doing?"

Paige tapped MUTE— "It's working—" she grinned.
UNMUTE. "We were going to do some work on our history
project, then a movie."

"Paige, I don't know if tonight's—"

"Here, Morgan wants to talk to you." MUTE. "Say exactly what I told you." She passed off her phone.

Morgan unmuted. "Hey, Mrs. Kingston."

"Hi, Morgan. How are you?" Ice.

"Y'know, coping the forty-five side of the fifteen good
days."

"This session's almost through."

"Siced," which meant, for no other reason than it did,
excited. "So, tonight: my mom's coming with; she told
me to text her digits to clear it."

Paige gave Morgan a thumbs up.

"I have your mother's *phone number* at home." Thaw-
ing.

Paige jabbed a downward finger at the air. Morgan:
MUTE.

"She's not going to call. Start driving."

Morgan pulled her sweet-sixteen sweet BMW Z4
from the curb.

"Get lots done," came Gwen's voice.

UNMUTE. "Fo-sho, Mrs. K."

"And tell Paige I'll expect her directly after the movie.
And thank your mom for me." Melted.

"You bet," came Morgan's peppy voice as Gwen noticed her two other daughters wave from the backseat. She looked to the street in time to watch the zippy little roadster zip past. Paige, reaching over from the passenger seat, tooted the horn. Gwen waved too, hiding sudden melancholy behind an offered smile.

Paige is already buh-bye.

An agitated sadness bore down on Gwen. Not over Paige's outburst this morning. Not from Michael's trouble. Not over the divorce. Maybe over how grown-up Paige and Morgan appeared in that flash of a passing second—how Paige would, one day soon, drive off for good.

If that boy's any indication—with someone I hate.

But that was fantasy. That was her mind selling her a cover story for the uneasiness her subconscious warning-flashed, but her preoccupations blinded her from registering. As the girls drove past, a silver Ford—the compact kind used exclusively by rental companies—pulled from its spot directly across the street from the academy. Looped an insistent U-turn. Its driver, a young man not so long from his teens himself: clean-cut, of flawless face and straight, hard jaw, chiseled and resolute. He set his rental on course for wherever Gwen's daughter and her reckless friend would lead.

If Gwen had seen the man, she would have done the double-take most people of her generation do. With his penetrating eyes, his disciplined charisma, he easily resembled a young Sidney Poitier. At first sight, people trusted and favored him. An edge in his kind of work.

It had already been a long day and tiring for Gwen. She'd staged a Falls Church Colonial for a July 4th weekend open house. The home was represented by an upstart and uppity real estate company Gwen's design group had contracted with at the beginning of June. It was an "audition" staging for Gwen and her team; if a sale came before August, the business this firm promised would bring her an extra ten, maybe as much as fifteen grand before New Year's.

Big help in view of the divorce.

Helluva day.

Gwen lengthened her back to spot-check the rearview mirror. Saw herself first. Her hair, a flat disaster. Shifted eyes to her daughters. "Charlotte, does Paige have a boyfriend?"

"You mean Deeb this morning?"

"What kind of name is that? *Deeb?*"

"They're not boyfriend-girlfriend."

Leigh shot Charlotte a dubious look. Charlotte shot back an elbow. Gwen shot down the road.

"Who is he?"

"Danny Boyington—D-B—Deeb for short. He skateboards. Does a YouTube channel."

"Must've missed it." Gwen huffed. "Does he have any brothers or sisters in your grades? Have I ever met his parents?"

Charlotte gave Leigh a look. *Bail me out.*

"Mom, can we stop for ice cream?" Leigh said with pigtailed innocence.

Eyes back to the rearview— "Charlotte, you want ice cream?"

"Turtle Mud in a cup. Extra nuts."

"Like your Daddy."

Charlotte looked at the street. Not going to get involved.

"What kind does Aunt Linny like?" said Leigh. "That's what I want."

The thaw Gwen had experienced with Paige welled tears in her eyes; she wouldn't think about Leigh growing up at all. Or anything Lynn might one day want.

Or require.

👑👑👑

LYNN PARKED her Porsche alongside Melody's truck. Burnished by the late afternoon sun, the summer heat shimmered off the Ram in waves.

Fire, redeem me...

Three words and the weight of Foxtail Farm—her family—to crush her spirit.

Should've all burned to the ground.

She quickly made her way across the lawn to the North Vista Outhouse, mollified to see Silas's move into the two-story guest house complete. Silas was at the far end of the lawn tossing the old football with Little Silas. He encouraged the boy with gentle words and laughter. Unlike he'd ever done with her.

"Hey, Melody," Lynn called from the base of the North Vista porch steps. Melody tossed a broad smile over her shoulder from where she washed the front windows. Vinegar-water and newspaper.

"Hi, hun." She stripped off her gloves. Skipped down the steps. Went for a tender hug. Lynn didn't like hugs—except from Melody whose hugs were undisguised. "Jack, come greet your Aunt Linny."

"Hi, Aunt Linny," Jack squeaked. "I'm washing windows!" To prove it, he balled a sheet of newsprint, drenched it, and proceeded to ruin the work his mother had just completed.

Melody sighed. "He's enthusiastic and I like to keep busy."

"Sobered up?" Silas said from behind.

Lynn faced him. Scruffed Little Silas's head. "Sorry. Was outta line."

Melody extended open hands. "Come on, boys, let's walk down to the beach like I promised."

Little Silas took one hand. Jack leaped from the porch. Tried to peel his brother's fingers free. "That's my hand!"

"It's mine!"

"One's just as good as the other," Melody said, slowly raising both out of reach. "Or are you trying to hurt my fingers' feelings?"

"Mine's the ring finger hand!" Little Silas insisted.

He must have been right because Jack immediately surrendered. Took the other. He shaped his face to make it look like he wasn't sad that the ring finger hand belonged to his twin. Silas noticed. His features clouded, a darkness he broke with a phony smile and a quick wink for Jack. His mom's right hand was just as good. Why wouldn't it be?

Melody lifted her eyes to the adults. "See you when we get back. Lynn, you staying to sup'?"

"We'll see." She waited until her sister-in-law was out of earshot. "I secured a Presidential Finding for covert action."

"As you should."

"Hal's team is rotating out of Manbij, Syria, end of the week. I shuffled some paperwork; he should already be wheels-down in Turkey."

"I hope you haven't done anything to jeopardize Hal's career."

"It'll probably earn him a medal."

Silas turned his attention to Melody and the twins now in the distance. They frolicked in the long-bladed beach grass Silas had allowed to climb the bluff and overrun the former tobacco fields.

"Look at my lambs!" he called.

Melody threw a hand over her head, painting the air with a wave without looking from the steep and weathered wooden stairs.

"Look at 'em," he softly repeated. He peered at his daughter. "Find dinner elsewhere. Their first night here will go unmarred."

"Wouldn't want it any other way."

Silas watched her stride purposefully back to her car. Pretending she looked nothing like Doris, he was able to ease the serpent coils twisted green around his black and heavy heart.

✦✦✦

A COOK-OUT FIRE blazed on a rounded point of Patuxent River shore known by locals as Fingernail Beach. As if pared from the sand, the moon stood upright in the darkened sky. Firelight tiger-striped a group of swim-suit-clad teenagers. Beer bongs. Jug wine. Hebrew National's. Mosquito whine. Burnt s'mores and dancing to Rhianna. Mosquitos slapped. Suds splashed, couples explored faces with lips, mouths with tongues, and Morgan perched, tan legs up like a cricket, on a driftwood log that was the color and texture of her glowing locks. Led a rambunctious game of "Zoom, Schwartz, Profigliano." Slapped mosquitos. Malibu shots in red Solo cups. Lost at it. Hit her coconut rum too hard. Sputtered.

"Fresh lager might help."

The British accent that accompanied the bottle over her shoulder was more than enough to grab Morgan's full attention. She turned. Turquoise eyes seductive. Took the beer from him. Lingered with her fingernails. He let her. His hand hanging like an austringer perching a peregrine.

"Aren't you the hottie?" she said. "Bet you have one of those sexy English-y names, huh?"

Mosquitos whined. Dive-bombed. Slapped.

"Seen Paige, luv?"

"Over in the sand piles with Deeb and some mini-Tanq's. They want privacy. C'mon, si'down. I'm jus' as fun to play with. It's not a hard game... Unless you want it to be. Who knows? You might get lucky."

He pinched a mosquito sucking blood from her arm. His lips spread in a grin. Mosquitoes zizzed in for more.

♕ ♕ ♕

THE DISTANT BONFIRE flashed green through the bottom of the miniature Tanqueray bottle Paige held to her eye. She turned it. The image distorted with the curve. With the thickness of the glass.

"Thiz loogs cool," said Paige. Barely. Half in the bag. Further into Deeb's lap. Reclined. Body loose against his as he sat cross-legged beneath her.

"Like a k'lei-dee'scope. Wanna see?"

Deeb "mmm'd." He moved his hands under Paige's bathing suit straps. Something Paige didn't notice until her top was down, and she gaped at her breasts. She laughed. Not because it was funny, not because she liked it, but because it startled her. She was embarrassed. And she was drunk. And he pulled her across his thighs. And he was laying her back in the sand. As delicately as he needed to do with a drunk girl—pretty much ungainly and thumpy—and he climbed over her, push-up position, cocked one leg, gave himself reach-down room. And Paige wasn't laughing now.

"Deeb. Don't. You—I, no, I changed m'mind." Paige squirmed.

"Babe, your body's screaming something entirely diff'."

Paige twisted. He pinned both her arms over her head with one hand. His other fiddled with the knot on his board shorts.

"Ga'dammit. Stop it!"

He covered her mouth with his. Slid fingers down her warm waist. Curled their tips under her bikini bottom waistline. Tugged.

Paige writhed. Bucked her pelvis. Flopped shoulders.

He clenched his fist around the string on her hip. Tugged harder. Twisted. Tried to rip it apart.

Paige beat the side of her leg along his muscular thigh. She bit his lip. He jerked his head back. She screamed but he pushed her cheek. Pushed her mouth into the sand.

He laughed at her. "You wanted to do this. You asked. This is—wha'is-it—? Con-sexual. You gotta learn to re-lax, babe."

He put all his strength into his wrist. Was going to have her bottoms off one way or the other. Until he wasn't. If God had intervened on Paige's behalf, reversed gravity, sent a cyclone to her aid, the only difference would have been the clarion call of heavenly trumpets to announce it. There weren't any trumpets. Just his gin-heavy breath. Her sand-choked cry. But that didn't mean Deeb wasn't unexpectedly weightless. He fell from her. Upward. Spun in the air. Flew away.

Paige's limbs reacted as if outside her own control. A gymnastic jackknife. She burst to her feet. Spit grit. Fell onto her bottom. Pedaled backwards, throwing sand with her heels. Watched her attacker crash onto a mound of branches, sticks, seagull feathers, and plastic trash. Scrabble and grope.

An older guy, not a cyclone at all—*but kinda, yeah?*—stepped toward her, hand outstretched. Kinda formal. Kinda not much older, kinda sweet-spot, just-right older.

And a different kind of embarrassment. Paige swiveled away. Her hands fumbled with her fallen top.

"I'm okay. Thanks. I'm just— Don't *look*—oh, I'm—oh, crap. I'm—" she gagged on a blast of vomit.

Bent over: coughing, drooling, blurry-eyed. Peering back, under her arm, Paige witnessed Deeb launch at the good-looking stranger who sipped from an open beer bottle. The guy didn't move—she couldn't see it—and he didn't spill a drop, even pause in the natural course of swallowing, yet Deeb was airborne again. He careened past her new champion in a somersault. Bowled into the beach grass that bound the sand to the black night woods behind them, alive and weird with creature sounds.

Deeb grabbed a heavy deadfall limb.

The stranger spoke softly. "That will end up breaking your legs. You'll never skate again, and I'm afraid you're not much good for anything else."

Paige wiped spittle with her forearm. Swished eyes between the two.

Deeb took a step in her direction. "Babe, you okay? Let's bounce from this douche."

"Ya'—bitch-bye."

"Look, I'm sorry. I really thought you—"

"This isn't the dune you want to die on, bruv. Hop to it."

Deeb shook the sand from his hair. Slunk into the woods. But for the whine of mosquitos, life within the darkness was stone silent at the curses of his passage.

The stranger squatted. Offered Paige his bottle.

"After what I just did? Ya'think?"

"It's only water. Might do you right."

Paige accepted the bottle. The water refreshed her mouth. Cooled her throat.

Simultaneously wanting to cry and confused why this guy had water in a beer bottle, Paige watched him pull a cellphone from his sweatshirt pocket. "Ring someone to take you home?"

The same soft, gentle voice—the musical accent, older, gorgeous, a chance like this happens only in movies, only with movie stars, only—

I've made an idiot of myself.

Her cheeks burned. She let him put his phone into her palm.

He stepped back. Gave Paige privacy. Paige dialed. The guy buried his hands in his front pouch pocket. Scanned the tree line. Scanned the shore. Both directions. Scanned the water.

Call answered, Paige turned away. Spoke quietly. "Morgan...? Yeah, I got sick. I need you to take me— No, *not* home— I'm friggin' trashed..."

Paige peered back toward the fire. She could see Morgan silhouetted against it. Slapping mosquitoes. Trudging her direction.

Paige cupped her mouth with her palm. "I dunno... Some British 'chap.' Black guy... *Yeah*, hella hot... Well, I dunno why he was looking for me. I never seen him before—" she glanced back to make sure he couldn't hear.

He couldn't. The man was gone.

Friday, July Second

1.

NOTHING ZAPS THE NOSE like the Turkish pines that populate the mountain forests south of Trabzon. In springtime, Michael hiked the lower trails the tourists trek to witness the vast carpets of Romuleas that briefly display pink and purple along the slopes. Burgundy in the vales. The invigorating tingle of an overwhelming peppermint fragrance that rides the breeze delights many into thinking they are enjoying the flowers' bouquet. They are mistaken. Sniffed up close, the Romulea releases a delicate honeysuckle aroma. Michael knew—having hiked the upper trails where there is only earth, rock, and tree—the crisp candy cane fragrance that fills the alpine air is exclusive and exquisite to the pines of Trabzon.

Exquisite, that is, until summer.

With summer, the sun's increased energy cooks the trees until pitch seams from their bark and harshens the minty sweetness into a bitter tingle with the pungency of urine. The hotter the days, the more latrine-like the stink. This foul piss-perfume of the Trabzon pines served as base for the nauseating odor that thickened the air inside the rear of the military truck. Diesel exhaust mixed with the rotten onion/stale tobacco tang

of Michael's unwashed guard. The truck climbed higher
into the wilderness, destined for a place above timber-
line where murder would be an open-air affair. Where
bodies went undiscovered, graves unclaimed, the stench
of human putrification unnoticed.

Up front, the lieutenant, who'd botched the coup
de grace on Father Cevik, had acquired a submachine gun—the American spy's one-way outing into the
mountains, his chance to redeem himself with Colonel
Vural. He'd checked his weapon's action eight times,
maybe ten, since the journey began. He smelled of gun
oil. Overcompensation for his weapon failure with the
priest. He clutched his gun-oil rag at his nose to com-
pensate for the rotten air.

Beside him, the driver—reeking as badly as his partner in the rear—grinned merrily, enjoying the drive away
from the drudgery of base. A Muslim fundamentalist,
everything had been going his way since they brought
in the priest. One infidel dead, the next soon; when the
work of the state matched the will of Allah, this was one
merry guy.

To be fair, Michael stunk a bit himself—dried blood
having an odor of its own—but what are you going to do,
chained to a bench, lurching up the steep switchbacks
of a mountain road on your way to get your head blown
off?

I hope you like to dig.

Michael's eyes fixed on the shovel held to the truck
bed by his guard's boots. His hands were cuffed, but
cuffed in front. His restraints paired to a floor chain.
Enough play in the slack—

Grab the shovel. Guard's throat—thrust/swipe. Windpipe severed—no scream.

No keys. Not this one. L-T's got 'em. Only get to kill one. Embarrass the lieutenant again. Infuriate the other into shooting me—

Least I won't have to dig. Never did like blisters.

The vehicle leveled into a stretch of forest. Michael chuckled. The guard considered him dully. He'd mellowed since he'd last worked Michael over with his baton. With his boots. His fists. With his stench.

Michael's eyes measured distance. Wrists weighed chains. Calculated: strength/heft/speed.

Shovel. Guard's throat: thrust/swipe/dead. Forget the keys: the baton. Lever the floor ring. Jump, roll, run.

The noncom fished a cigarette pack from his tunic. Shook free a stick—

Baton through the ring—lever. Tip of the shovel—prybar for the ring's bolt plate?

—lipped it from the pack. Shook out the end of another. Offered to Michael.

Michael responded. *"Olmasa iyi olur. Sigaranın sağlığıma zararlı olduğunu duydum."* Better not. I hear cigarettes are bad for my health.

Got a laugh on the cloud of sheepshit smoke as the guard worked the cigarette to business.

The driver slammed brakes. The guard's smile vanished. Michael pitched sideways as the truck shuddered/rattled/stopped.

Michael snatched the shovel.

👑👑👑

THE CAB. The lieutenant: Arm braced against the dashboard. Scowled at a tree across the narrow road. Oily rag quivered in his fingers.

The driver: *"Kesildi."* It's been cut.

The lieutenant snatched the radio mic.

Two soundless, tiny flashes from the covering trees ahead.

👑👑👑

MICHAEL'S GUARD SHOUTED. Seized the shovel handle before Michael could swing its blade. Tug-a-war. Michael—a quick two-plus-two—released it. Guard catapulted back. Tossed shovel out of reach. Furious. Shouted to his lieutenant. No answer. Did the math himself.

"Second thought, I will have that cigarette." And because a shade of cruelty ran in Michael's bloodline: *"Senden biraz daha uzun yaşayacağım dostum."* Going to live a little longer than you, my friend.

The guard lunged for the rear hatch. Michael barely winced as a third bullet blew through his guard's chest.

Seconds later, the rear hatch whipped wide.

"American! Don't shoot!" Michael stared at a helmeted and night vision-masked paramilitary who aimed a submachine gun equipped with thermal imaging at his nose.

"Not like there haven't been times."

"Hal?"

Hal Kingston spoke into his throat mic. "Vehicle clear. Jawbone secure."

"Jawbone?"

"Operation DEMBONES. Be grateful for Jawbone; I got 'Coccyx.' Whatever the hell that is."

Michael could see two more CIA clandestine Spec-Fors—dudes kitted out to the max, faces anonymous behind NVGs—advance to secure the cab. A third climbed past Michael— "S'cuse me, sir." Gave the guard a head-tap. Gray matter/dark blood. Rifled his rig.

Michael returned his gaze to his younger brother. "'Coccyx' means 'assbone,' Assbone."

The first pair reappeared, one with the lieutenant's key. Freed him.

"Glad to see Lynn's kept her sense of humor about this." Hal gave his brother a hand. "You smell like shit."

"Gotta love the smell of this forest, though, right?"

"Zombie piss?"

A radio crackled inside the cab. Voice: Turkish.

"What's the word?" said Hal.

"Must be GPS on the vehicle. They're asking why we stopped."

Hal's three men gathered. Faced Michael. Spooky. Emotionless in their tech.

Hal said, "Ready to hump it?"

One of them tossed Michael the Turkish lieutenant's SMG. Almost slipped from his grip. Michael checked the load and its action. Rubbed excess oil across the dead guy's thigh. Once—not enough—again, and "Let's do this."

2.

THE WRAPAROUND PORCH AT Foxtail Farm was the only living space Silas allowed the family to gather. Or friends and colleagues—those he no longer entertained; those whom he browbeat, embarrassed, or generally made uncomfortable when he had. A hard and fast "peculiarity"—better written, m-a-d-n-e-s-s—going on since Hal's mother Doris died from cancer.

Melody pulled open the plantation shutters to welcome the dawn.

At least "cancer" is what Hal told her. He might have misspelled that too, as, once, Gwen—over an uncorked white zinfandel and her uncorked yap—swore Melody to secrecy before telling her it was "m-u-r-d-e-r." Then instantly blabbered "S-T-F-U, Gwen," and pretended she'd never spelled a word.

Melody knew: For the dead, what made them that way didn't matter at all. Suffering ends. Dead is dead. The darkness—

wooden ships, iron chains, a place without light

—existed beyond words. Whatever had happened to Doris—or hadn't—didn't matter to Melody or Melody's place in this family she'd come to love as the only family she'd ever known.

Out with the dark.

Bring sunlight to Foxtail Farm. Be the Kingston light.

A purpose worthy of my mother.

Yes. What Melody was good at. Sunshine. Longed her whole life to prove it. Now, among the Kingstons, she did.

Silas had given no specific rules on which rooms Melody and the kids—and Hal, when he returned from combat (no use telling her he ever did anything but)—might or might not occupy now that the manor house was theirs. But Melody respected Doris's spirit. She'd notice it. Now and then. In the mirrors. Just around the corners. A spirit distinctly separate from the Doris of the stairway portrait. Melody would swear it was Doris's insistence which bedrooms, which dressing room—

"Silas, what am I s'posed with a dressing room?"

"Make it lovely by walking into it. Or desolate by not."

—and which bathrooms would be fine by her, but day-living—all of it, when up and out of bed and time to be counted—yes, Silas had been correct, and Doris demanded: day-living took place on the porch.

Snap, snap, snap. Melody worked her way along the north side of the house—shutter slats, *snap.* She made the turn into the east gallery, which extended off the dining room and the kitchen. Here the shutters were open as she'd left them last night. A view across the lawn to the two-story detached building Melody saw as a second house—better, second mansion—but which the rest of them considered guest quarters and Silas, ridiculously, called the Outhouse. Silas's new home.

Silas wasn't there. Sat on the steps below her. Looked forlorn... until the screen door creaked and Melody poked her head outside.

"You could have come in," she said. "I left it unlocked last night for you."

"Don't. There's burgling. Anyway, I didn't want to surprise you. It's your home now."

"'Burgling?' As in burglars?"

"Who else burgles?"

Melody amused. Swung the old-fashioned, wood-framed door wide. "You're silly."

"Make sure Hal tightens that turnbuckle. It'll stop the squeak. Door sags on the top hinge." He pecked her cheek because she'd lifted it. He came inside.

She studied Silas. Fond of Silas. Concerned for Silas. "You look a bit ragged, Papa. Coffee?"

"Didn't sleep."

"You never do."

"How would you know that?"

"I nursed nights down here before Hal and I got the condo. I could hear you stomping around."

"Wasn't me. Never stomped in my life."

"I'll get that coffee..."

Melody stepped around him for the French doors into the kitchen where she'd started a pot.

"Melody, you are the best thing that ever happened to this family. You're our angel. I'm fit-and-fine this morning, but there is a situation. It involves your husband. Let's walk before the lambs arise?"

Melody stilled at the trouble in his voice. She wasn't fearful; in fact, where Hal was concerned, Melody never experienced anxiety in the slightest. And she appreciated that—unlike with Gwen and Michael—when Silas referred to Hal, he used "husband" rather than his son's name; he always said "Michael" with Gwen, keeping claim of his firstborn for himself.

♔ ♔ ♔

GWEN EXITED HER VOLVO beside Melody's truck. She'd seen Melody and Silas with their coffees, watching the twins cavort in the fields. They'd seen her. The shirtless boys waved skinny arms with the fervor of castaways sighting a ship. She paused between the vehicles to check her face in the truck's jumbo sideview mirror. She'd cried all night, and Gwen double-checked that the indications were gone.

They weren't.

Two days running, babe. You're losing it.

She plastered on her most pleasing face. Stepped out across the lawn to meet Melody and Silas, the embodiments of her envy and her pain.

"Gwen. Michael's going to be fine. You *know* that." Melody folded Gwen into easy arms.

"As if I needed this on top of that."

Melody squinted.

"It's Paige. Tell me she's here."

"She is not." Silas raked Gwen with Tommy gun eyes. Found her wanting. As usual. "Get ahold of yourself."

"How? My baby didn't come home."

Shit. Here I go. All I need for him to see.

But Gwen couldn't help it. She sobbed.

"Your nephews are standing right there. Stop that."

Melody snapped Silas a stern look.

He eased up. "The girl's eighteen in a week. Hell, Paige is probably home and gone, the time you wasted coming here."

"I called her friend's mother. She never went there."

Melody's thumbs gently wiped Gwen's tears. "I can't imagine. You should have come sooner."

"I knew the reception I'd get."

Silas stepped back. The twins scampered over. They usually liked looking at Aunt Gwen, but at the sight of her woe, they clustered alongside Silas. He put a hand on each of their shoulders and pronounced, "Fact. Teenage girls who stay out late Friday night always turn up before noon Saturday. Rarely later than Sunday."

"Something you know from Lynn?" Gwen rasped.

Melody dropped her gaze.

"From my son. Michael. The number of his girlfriends I've seen carrying shoes out those gates..." Shook his head, though his eyes never left Gwen's.

Gwen wished she were more like Melody, who scoffed easily at Silas—his thundering and threatening reduced to peskiness. But Gwen couldn't brush off Silas's remarks. There were times she considered what his face might look like as a skull.

👑 👑 👑

THE DESCENDING BLACKHAWK *whup-whupped* its arrival onto the plateau. Hal's heavy weapons operator, code-name Headbone, was there. Ahead. Securing the LZ. He sighted through his machine gun's night-optics. "I'm crosshairs-on seven heavily armed, ripshit Mehmets S-20-east and one klick out, kicking rocks our way. Hose 'em now while they're bunched; no one walks, no one's the wiser."

Dirt and small stones, sticks and dead scrub, scattered around him in helicopter downdraft.

"Hold at REDCON-1," Hal replied as he and the others gathered among the rocks and dwarf pines at the plateau base. "Do not. Repeat. Do not make first contact. Making our ascent now."

"Wilco," said Headbone. Covered the hostiles. Finger itchy. Ready to throw heat.

Hal and the one called Legbone—SpecOp who bumped-off Michael's guard—climbed. Staggered themselves in position to assist Michael. The last operator, codename Footbone, covered the rear from the base. Prone. Weapon zeroed on their pursuit. Shielded behind a low mound of dug earth and stone. Last of about ten mounds they'd already moved through.

Five minutes back:

Michael: "Coulda just waited here for me, and I wouldn't a'had to walk."

Hal: "You got pussyboy hands. You'd a'gotten blisters digging one of these, and we'd a'had to listen to you bitching the whole way home."

The Turkish unit, under Colonel Vural's lead, spread out. Opened fire on the plateau. On the helicopter, dull black in the moonlight.

Oblique to the bird, Headbone responded. Brass ripped. Tracers streamed. Drew fire away from the aircraft. From his team. From Jawbone.

Michael mounted the stone face.

Hal: "Grab my hand. I'll relay you."

Shouts preceded enemy gunfire carving toward them.

Hal strained. "Come on!" But Michael dropped. Into the rocky cover at plateau base.

Footbone teed off with his M27. Launched a 40mm grenade from its M203 tube. Threw out suppressing fire.

Hal folded into a crevice. Hal made himself small. Only his arm exposed. Hal, harsh: "Michael?!"

"Gotta climb another way! Don't let 'em chew you up! Go!" Michael charged his submachine gun. Crouched beside Footbone. Michael said: "Tell me there's another route."

Footbone gave a sharp nod. Into his mic— "Coccyx: be advised, moving with Jawbone to fallback."

Hal's voice returned: "Affirmative. When we light their position, pop smoke, and beat feet."

Michael covered in the rocks behind Footbone. Watched Legbone, followed by Hal, clear the headwall. Mount the plateau. Roll across its lip. Add bursts to Headbone's long-tempo lead. Brass flying. Hot. Scattered. Constant rain of fire.

Footbone popped a canister. "Smoke out!" Grabbed Michael's shoulder. Guided west.

Topside: Hal slapped Legbone's tac-vest. "Load up! Go!"

Legbone dashed for the Blackhawk.

An RPG round *wooshed* past. Beneath the helicopter's tail. Exploded rocks.

More rocket-propelled grenades. *Bam! Bam! Bam!* Miss. Near miss. Almost not.

Hatch crewman: "We need to get airborne!"

Legbone: "Don't you lift off!" Into mic: "Coccyx: bird's taking fire!"

Footbone and Michael hit the second pitch. A heavy grunt. Footbone wounded. Footbone down. Above: Hal's face.

Beside Hal: Headbone, re-setting gun. Headbone: re-setting trigger-finger. Muzzle blast. Hot brass. Re-setting the Turks' advance. Tracer arcs. Smoking brass. Re-setting opportunity. Re-setting time.

"Michael: now!"

Michael dropped. Again. Dashed to Footbone. Again. Grabbed his rig— "You're going up!" Yanked Footbone to his feet.

"Better I cover from here, sir!"

"Bullshit." Michael hauled him to the rock wall. "You don't give this your all, you're gonna get me killed." Michael pushed Footbone from behind.

Footbone bled. Footbone climbed. Michael guided/shoved.

Hal extended for Footbone—gloved hand empty, fingers wide, grasping air.

Footbone dripping all over Michael's neck. Michael strained his shoulder under Footbone's ass. Strained his back to jack Footbone higher.

Crescendo of yells. The opposing force. A second unit. Link-up. Both push forward. Heavy fire. All see: overwhelming force/ultimate kill.

Headbone rolled from his gun. Assists Hal: Footbone hauled over the rim.

"Get him to the bird!" Hal ordered. Hal rolled back for his brother.

Gunfire shredded rock face. Michael: gone.

Michael's voice: "Hal! Take off! Only thing that'll distract 'em from me!"

"No! Coming to you!"

"Don't fucking dare!" Time-freeze between brothers.

"We won't leave without you!"

"If you stay—"

"Won't leave a man behind!"

"If you fucking stay: they'll know I'm still here!"

Hal pounds: fist-into-earth. Michael shouts: "You saved my life already, but you gotta let me go!"

Fist-into-earth. "Fuck that!" Fist. Earth. Agony.

👑👑👑

READY TO DESCEND, *Hal seized from behind by Legbone. "Down there's suicide, sir! We lost him! I'm sorry!"*

"He isn't lost!"

As if in answer, traveling up the plateau from darkness below come faint words. Hal's name. A statement. Maybe a promise. Maybe a goodbye. A final "I love you, brother!"

The groundfire increases in ferocity, lighting both Hal and Legbone's faces.

Sudden, brief silence.

Escape silence?

Death silence?

Gone silence. More ripping lead. More tracers. More rockets. Kingdom come shitstorm.

"Michael? MICHAEL!"

✧ ✧ ✧

LEGBONE GRABBED HIS CAPTAIN. Ignored Hal's struggle against him. Ignored protest. Ignored orders. Hustled through the whirlwind of dirt. Of stinging stone. Of singing lead. Crashed both their bodies into the waiting chopper.

Gunfire. Swarming Turks. Rockets. *Boom! Bam! Boom!*

The Blackhawk torqued into the air.

Hal screamed over rotor blast. "Go back for him!"

"Captain: he's gone." Legbone pushed him further inside. Blocked the hatch.

"No! He said, 'I'm gonna be fine!'"

Legbone met his squadmates' eyes. Shook his head. Not what he heard. Not fucking-at-all. Out of enemy range, they fled from the Valley of Dry Bones.

3.

THREE TAPERS TIPPED IN flame. Crème-colored candles seated in early American silver candlesticks. Their flickering repeated in the dozens of impressions cast about the mirrors inside the Foxtail Farm formal dining room. Hopscotched to the house interiors beyond. An illusion of luminosity. Faces duplicated with the candle flames and their bouncing light: Silas, Gwen, Melody—seated at three of four place-settings at Doris's massive, elliptical dining table—allow, in reflections, Foxtail Farm manor to appear filled by a party that isn't. Tricky thing about mirrors: they mimic life marvelously, but even at Foxtail Farm where with one glance you can recreate yourself one hundred times in an instant, the glasses remain empty of vitality.

The three adults at table were somber and without company. While, adjacent to house proper, beneath the electric lights of the porch, Charlotte, Leigh, Jack, and Little Silas were cocooned and contained perfectly with one another away and unseen by the light/life-stealing glass (that isn't silver, but the purest white of all)—grinning, quietly goofing, kids.

Melody served a slow cooker roast and simple stovetop potatoes with carrots and leeks. Her food—as always—delicious. She seasoned it with a concoction of southern spices, a recipe from her vague and itinerant past. Secrets she wouldn't divulge. Conversation was light after grace as loud appetites settled to nourishment.

"Mom...?" Paige's voice quavered from the darkness.

Gwen quivered; a harp string plucked. Her unruly hands grabbed the table's edge to rise.

"Don't, Gwen." Silas. "She must come to you for control."

Gwen nervous. Mouth buttoned.

"Hi." Paige from the doorway.

Yesterday's school outfit rumpled. Eyes ringed from lack of sleep. From alcohol. "Mom. I am so sorry."

Gwen sprang from her high-backed chair. Held Paige. Cheek pressed cheek.

"I was so pissed—sorry, Papa—I mean angry. At you. And I was having fun—*for once*—and then it was too late, and I—I—I don't know what you want me to say."

"Shh... I was awake all night, I was so worried. You scared me, Li'l Bean."

"'Li'l Bean?'" said Silas. "She's not two."

Melody placed her napkin aside. "C'mon, let's us fix you a plate." She herded Gwen and Paige to the kitchen.

"How ya been, Paige?" Jack and Little Silas crowed from the porch, gleeful and excited. Charlotte and Leigh, clever instigators, cracked up.

"That'll do, lambs."

Melody returned alone from the kitchen. Resumed her seat.

Silas cupped his mouth. "Ladies, we are waiting."

A moment. Gwen and Paige came into view on the porch. Paige pulled a chair to the children's table. Her mother prattled. "Girls, scoot-scoot. Make room, please."

"Paige," Silas.

"Papa?" Paige.

"You sit with the adults now." He pointed to the place beside him, already set.

"Aunt Lynn's spot?"

Silas's eyes locked with Lynn's reflection in a hallway mirror. "I see an empty chair. Take it."

Lynn pretended she hadn't met her father's gaze. She lurched into the room.

"Didn' mean'ta be late." Hammered drunk. Swung in the direction of the kitchen. "Oh... Hal foun' Michael. And Hal's gon-be fine. Yep. He's comin' home. Mike's..."

"Some wine?" Silas's teeth gleamed. "Give it to her. Now."

Melody took a protective gulp from her goblet before handing it to Lynn. Lynn finished it with a single belt.

"What about Michael?" Gwen. "Lynn: tell me!"

"I'm sorry, Gwen. You guys. Kids. I din mean t'do it this way..."

"Give her another one."

"I won't, Silas." Melody's soft hand—the empty glass—Lynn's shaky fingers.

"Don' nee'nymore."

"Done drinking? Fine. Now face this family. Explain what you have done to your brother."

Lynn fought against the swaying of the room. "He wanted to say, 'Thank you.' An' I lied 'bout that an' I lost him."

Gwen ashen. Charlotte and Leigh stared. Horror eyes. Horror pale.

"Aunt Lynn, what are you saying?" whispered Paige.

Lynn looked at her niece. All the children. Her mind spun. The least of it from alcohol. Her voice ran from her, and Lynn had a dizzying vision of her mother, long ago, calling her name, shrouded by smoke, orange-cast by fire; of Michael—bare feet pounding river sand—shrieking at her as a ran away with her mirrored toy. And Lynn said: "A kaleidoscope turns on itself."

"What did you say?" Silas. Warning. Hard.

She stared at him, sensed the demon of her past, present, her future, possess her. "I said, 'Michael has vanished.'"

But that wasn't what she'd said. She waited for Silas's ridicule. For everything. Past. Present. Future come.

Silas dabbed his lips with his napkin. "Absurd. No one vanishes."

Saturday, July Third

1.

A LREADY HOT, THE MORNING flamed through the open window of the upstairs dressing room. Room and window opened by Melody, borrowed by Gwen who sat behind Paige before the vanity mirror: Heirloom. Colonial. Servant-made. Mother and daughter cast in the essence of morning's fire. For the last time in Paige's childhood, Gwen brushed her daughter's amber hair.

"Papa's right. People don't vanish."

"Sweetie, that was just Papa taking advantage of a bad word choice so he could pick on your Aunt Linny."

"It's lame how he does that. He picks on Aunt Lynn because she drinks, but Aunt Lynn drinks because Papa picks on her."

"Aunt Linny's drinking belongs to Aunt Linny."

"As if."

Gwen stopped brushing. Locked eyes with her daughter in reflection. "Paige, I need you to promise: Never mention 'divorce' about me and Daddy. To Papa. To anyone else."

"Oh. You mean lie?"

"No. Daddy and I spoke the other night. Before all this. We fixed things."

Paige curled her lip. "'Final Judgment on Dissolution of Marriage'? No need to Google what that fixes."

Gwen examined the hairbrush. "We decided not to accept it."

"Really? You can do that?" Paige stared, eyes daring her mother to meet them again.

"I swear. Yes."

But she didn't look back.

"We're all hoping for the best, Paige, but if your father *is* dead, a divorce becomes a financial complication. You, your sisters—"

"You say 'dead.' Like that. Like it's so easy. Like—"

Paige! I'm barely holding my shit together!

Calm. She's a child. My child.

"You and your sisters and I: all we have is each other, and there are expenses and—"

"Wrong."

Gwen's eyes bugged. *How is that possibly wrong?*

"My sisters and me? *We'll* still be Kingstons."

Gwen stood back. Slapped the hairbrush in her palm. "I think that will do."

She dropped a black rubber band into her eldest daughter's hand. "Pull it back. Booze is terrible on hair."

♕ ♕ ♕

GWEN AND HER DAUGHTERS wore red, white, and blue summer dresses for church. Charlotte in polka dots; Paige, floral bouquets tied with blue ribbons; Leigh in bric-a-brac-pattern stripes with Alice in Wonderland shoulder puffs. These three met with Silas's approval.

At the other end of the patriotic dress code, Gwen wore a tight, knit thing, white with a blue field over her chest, white stars suggesting pasties, and wavy, red stripes running from her right shoulder to her left thigh that, separately, looked like fingers attempting to lift her hem for a game of diddle-me-this.

"How nice," said Silas through a smile shaped like a gutting knife.

Gwen wiggled eyebrows.

Eat shit, you old bird.

They joined Melody and the twins, waiting on the garden lawn in front of the family chapel.

"You boys have better things to do than gawk at your aunt. Go pull weeds." Silas gestured the twins aside.

"You all look lovely." Melody to the rescue. "I'm going to want to get a picture with everyone."

She wore white. The white cotton sack dress from Target with the yellow stripe they'd all seen her in at Easter.

Gwen wiggled eyebrows.

You got the house, you got the fancy truck, and still playing "poor me."

Melody pinned a simple red, white, and blue ribbon over her heart. "There," she said. Her hair, in a bun, glowed where summer had kissed the ends of her dark curls bronze.

Sun in a bottle's what that is.

Stop it, Gwen. Sisters.

Silas stepped behind Melody. Claimed Melody's shoulders with his hands before saying past her ear, "Just to prepare you, Gwen, today's priest is female."

Unexpected. Gwen cocked her head at Melody.

"Vivianne Tremelin. She's lovely." Melody smiled.

Her sons wandered to a clump of dandelions.

"More importantly," Silas said, "God speaks through this woman. I will entertain no comments on past remarks I've made about women wearing vestments." With that, he moved off to join his grandsons blowing wishes.

Paige pulled her phone. Clustered with her sisters.

"You know the rules, Paige!"

"Mom: church selfies promote Christianity."

Melody touched Gwen's arm, distracting her. Leaned in. "You tell me, but I think Silas and the Reverend have a thing going."

...*My faaaavorite sister.* "Tell *me*. What do you know? Every detail. Don't hold out on me, sis'." Gwen squeezed in close.

👑 👑 👑

THE DIOCESAN CHAPLAIN, Reverend Vivianne Tremelin, stark in her black blouse, clerical collar, and gray skirt, waited for Lynn to park and join her on the gravel path.

"Good morning, Lynn. I've missed you here these last few Saturdays. And you're not showing up in town on Sundays."

Lynn made side-eye, less sarcastic than amused. No drinks in her. Yet. Weight of her bangle.

Slip inside for a pop?

You're an embarrassment.

And isn't that the point?

They took the path around the North Vista Outhouse. The moment soon with God: He knew what she thought. Knew her heart, fractured as it was. He offered strength, which Lynn countered with the strength to deny it—80 proof—and could pretend—*live your cover*—it made her good.

"The world doesn't appear to be on fire." Vivianne's eyes twinkled. "Maybe you're seeing someone? Dating?"

"Vivi: when I take a day off from *my* calling, fires catch."

"Ah. Another Kingston carrying the globe for the rest of us. The apple doesn't fall far from the tree."

"This apple rotted right off that tree—Long. Time. Ago."

They joined the others. Lynn forced cheerfulness. Gestured as if presenting the priest on stage. "Ms. Vivianne Tremelin. Your Kingston flock."

Silas stepped forward, offering his hand. "Thank you, Vivianne. You light our Saturdays."

"That would be the presence of the Lord. But I pitch in."

She took his hand. Silas added his other. Handshake to hand cuddle.

Lynn's notice traveled from their hands to her sisters-in-law. Faces. Expressions. All she needed to know. Mouthed, *They're fucking?*

One smirk. One arched set of eyebrows. Confirmed.

Lynn laughed out loud. Covered by pulling Leigh, her niece, into a playful hug. "I've never seen you so pretty—except *every day* since you came out of mommy's tummy."

Leigh giggled. Leigh wiggled. Gwen smiled pleasantly at Lynn, who handed off her child, and pretended the somersault inside her tummy wasn't an echo of what might have been.

Almighty God, unto whom all hearts are open, all desires known...

♛ ♛ ♛

45,000 FEET ON HIGH over the Atlantic. Forward cabin of the CIA 737 aircraft divided into cubicle spaces where debriefers questioned Hal and his team.

"Jawbone yelled, 'Hal: I'm gonna be fine. I love you, brother.' Definitely confident. Already disengaged. Withdrawing from the firefight. Relatively safe."

"You saw him moving away?"

"I know that he was."

"Did you visually acquire him?"

"No."

"Is it possible, Captain, you misheard?"

Cleanse the thoughts of our hearts by the inspiration of thy Holy Spirit...

"I know what I know."

"Yes, or no?"

"No."

The debriefer consulted notes. Made one of his own. Added the timecode from the recorder. "Is it possible Michael might have said, 'Hal: I'm gonna *die?*'"

"Did one of my teammates tell you that?"

"It's my question. Did Michael say, 'Hal: I'm gonna die?'"

Rotor-wash dust-up. Muzzle flash and tracers. Hot brass. Rocky jumble below. Michael calling up and back, "I'm gonna be fine! I love you, brother!"

Calling up/calling back.

Voice: separating it. From chopper noise. From gunfire. From RPGs. From the patter-clatter of tumbling brass: "I'm gonna die! I love you, brother!"

"No, sir. Not possible." Hal shut his eyes.

That we may perfectly love thee...

"I'm going to die, brother!"

Opened them. Closed/open: either way, he couldn't see what he wanted. Closed/open: hadn't seen what he didn't want. Distinct/indistinct.

And worthily magnify thy holy Name...

"Not possible at all, sir." Didn't know. Looked his debriefer dead in the eye. "I'd like to be done answering questions."

He watched the debriefer write a few sentences before switching off his recording device. "You've done well. And I'm sorry for your loss."

Through Christ our Lord. Amen.

"Don't be. Michael isn't dead."

♛♛♛

PAIGE FOCUSED ON VIVIANNE TREMELIN breaking the consecrated bread. "Alleluia. Christ our Passover is sacrificed for us."

The assembled Kingstons responded: "Therefore, let us keep the feast. Alleluia."

Papa first, Paige's family filed to the altar to receive the sacraments. Paige knelt beside Aunt Lynn. Formed her hands to receive. Said a prayer inside her head.

Dear God, I'm sorry for my lies. I'm sorry for my bad behavior. My sins. Getting drunk—Okay? Punish me in as many ways as you want but save Dad. And if there ever was a time I needed a sign you hear me: make it now? Today. Please-please. Please. I've prayed a lot. I'll pray more—and thank you—and—please—Amen.

Paige watched Lynn. Lynn swallowed her piece of the communion bread—

Bet Aunt Melody baked it this morning...

—but when the chalice was offered, Aunt Lynn crossed her arms over her chest. She did not drink. Bowed and allowed the cup to pass.

Later. After a final prayer. After Lynn rushed off to Langley. After the baked French toast Melody prepared the previous night and set to baking before the service. After Silas tucked an offering inside Vivianne's purse and walked the priest to her car (where Paige watched him kiss her goodbye—*hella big* kiss). After that—whatever *that* was—her family relaxed on the eastern length of the porch.

The porch: a mismatch of sofas and chairs. Pillows and throws. Coffee tables. A game table. A puzzle table. Cozy bright. Bookcase. DVD tower. Television. Liquor cabinet/wet bar. Most unlike Silas in comfort and in warmth, but then again, he had furnished it and he wasn't someone else.

Melody cleared plates and loaded the dishwasher. Gwen gathered sheets and comforters from their *"Can't we stay the weekend?"* sleepover. Bundled them. Set them aside for someone to deal with later.

Charlotte played *Chutes and Ladders* with the twins. The boys laughed hysterically as she fell from the lead, punished by landing on the "stealing oranges" slide.

Leigh lifted a hardbound and heavy, illustrated copy of T.H. White's *The Once and Future King* from its bookstand, presented one Christmas—or so Michael had told Paige—from Silas to her grandmother, who'd cried to receive it, though later said it had been from joy. Leigh walked the book to Silas.

Paige observed him from the dim threshold between the darkened sitting room of empty mirrors and the family porch. Seated in a wing-back chair, his lips propped on the knuckles of his folded hands, he observed his younger grandchildren with unguarded peacefulness. For the first time in her life, Paige felt herself apart from this family. She felt as though she might float away. Felt as though she might burst into tears over—

Deeb? Not that! Who cares? I'm fine.

Dad? Daddy?

No one vanishes.

Why didn't Aunt Lynn drink the wine. Christ's blood?

Thanks a lot. What am I supposed to do with that, God?

No. Not that. All that/*none* of that. That stuff wasn't going to be it. And yet, since the night before, since she'd not been punished, since she'd not spoken of her assault by Deeb and knew she never would, since she'd been rescued by a stranger who knew her name but shouldn't; since she'd so easily cut her mother from their family that morning and it didn't bother her in the slightest—unless her mother refused to change; since she knew her future would take her from all of them and had been coming fast against her: Paige had not allowed herself any time to appreciate what the future, hurtled into, would force her to leave behind. What the future would take from her. Make vanish forever. This. What she'd always had and held granted.

The house behind her was cold. The air, heavy, pressed urgent hands against her back. Paige inched forward onto the porch. Inched into a patch of sunlight streaming through the shutters. She found a Kingston smile and made her face useful with it.

Silas said to Leigh, "Thata girl. Our favorite book."

Silas pulled Leigh into his lap. Paige had shared the exact moment many times before.

How far back did it go?

A sudden vision of Lynn as the girl in the place of her little sister.

And it wasn't a vision—they looked so similar. Not like Gwen at all. The cruel Kingston part of Paige imagined how much Leigh's Kingston attributes bothered a woman as vain as her mother.

"Papa, do the voices!" Leigh cried.

He found their bookmark. "Only if you start off as Wart."

"'Well,' said the Wart, 'what about it?'" Leigh intoned a little English chirp.

"What-ho?! Brilliantly rendered."

Leigh snuggled against his strong chest. Silas took the voice of Merlyn. Paige knew the passage by heart. Where Merlyn puffs and blows. About what is best for being sad.

It was only now Paige appreciated that time rode the back of sadness. This realization, whatever it meant—and Paige had no earthly idea beyond the thought-words: *time is sadness*—embodied itself in the constriction of her throat.

Silas paused. Eyes drawn from the page. He glanced at Paige.

They shared a look.

She wished she would not grow up. Wished time would move her to live backwards. Backwards like Merlyn. Wished safety, happiness; wished ignorance. Wished she'd prayed for that.

The one-time important drink: Why did Aunt Linny refuse the chalice?

"Remember when you sat here?"

Paige reflected: while Papa's shortcomings as a father were plentiful, they dissolved under the perfection he had achieved as a grandfather.

Paige was a Kingston. She nodded, *I remember, Papa.* She swallowed honest emotions and presently helped herself back to herself. She felt nothing but the smile affixed to her face. And she pictured the stranger's—her champion's—kind face, concern, when he'd given her his phone.

He'll have to call to get it back.

A token upstairs in her purse. Inside the room where she slept. Beside the bed where she dreamed. Within the dream where she flew in an airless, starry sky. She was kissing him; she was warm, Paige safe in his strange arms, safe in the fireworks explosions surrounding them in waterfall decorations of fire.

Where passion whispers, love makes time irrelevant.

2.

WHEN THE CIA OLD Headquarters Building was designed, the architects purposely conceived the windows to resemble the arrow-slits of a medieval castle. Thick and soundproofed, they contain a field of white noise generated between their double-panes to prevent electronic eavesdropping. Lynn found the whole set-up a dirty trick on sunlight as well. Did something invisible, something wrong to it.

"I took the initiative to distribute Michael's identity to airports." She moved the vase of beach glass, adjusting the prismatic spray away from DDO Gravin's face.

"Appreciated." In weekend casual, he leaned in the doorway that connected her office to his outer suite.

"My words or the glare?"

She stood behind her desk, her hands wide and flat on its surface, fingers splayed, like a duelist, ready to draw at the slightest provocation. Her eyes bore into his.

"Lynn: I understand follow-through and faith, but the returns from the DEMBONES debriefs..." He shook his head. "I am not hopeful. You shouldn't get—"

"I've gotten a passport match in Athens." Lynn lifted two photographs.

He lifted an eyebrow, narrowed the other eye—surprise, meet skeptical, meet...flirty? Lynn had other biometrics to worry about. She came around her desk. Gary shut the door. Moved inside to meet her. The first photo was a passport picture. Clearly, Michael Kingston.

"What identity kit is he using?"

"His Canadian cover passport with the 'Arthur Danford' legend."

"How the hell'd he get that?"

"He must have stashed it. Before his capture. Somewhere ahead of the chase. Like he knew."

"There's something you're not telling me."

Their eyes met. His: curiosity. Hers: blank.

"Did Michael give you some indication he was following a plan in all of this?"

"I've no idea what Michael is doing, what he's done, or how he's done it."

A Kingston buries guilt. She handed Gary the second photograph. "This next is Michael moving through Greek passport control."

"Presumably Michael."

The image appeared to be her brother, although his face was tilted downward. Hair forward, fallen and obscuring; features barely visible as he tucked his chin to examine his passport the moment the photo was taken. It might not have been Michael at all, but Lynn insisted: "My brother couldn't get around having to use the passport."

"But he knew enough to hide his face from the camera."

"In any event—biometric recognition of the quarter-profile lands a sixty-eight percent positive I-D."

Gary went to her white sofa. Paced in front of it a few steps. Looked back. "They stopped him. Yes?"

"As our Athens Chief of Station put it, 'Greek Immigration Control always has a dozen perfect reasons for doing exactly the wrong thing.'"

"Where is he now?"

"Apparently... headed back here."

Gary swished his gaze between the photos, then directly onto Lynn's face. "Convincing..."

"As in, 'convinced?'"

"As in 'the process of being.' He's working from an escape kit. You know, that means he's planned this. *All* of it. Layered it with contingencies."

"I'd say Cevik isn't the end. I'd say losing Cevik was the beginning."

"Lynn, is this your brother?" Gary wagged the second photo.

"I gave him that exact jacket. Christmas. And who else but Kingstons sport black-gold wedding rings?"

Gary inflated his cheeks.

Lynn leaned against her desk. Picked up a file. Held it close. "I've written a Presidential Finding to run Dulles International as a covert operation. Just need your sig'."

She extended the folder. Gary waved it off. "It'll take too long. Have to include FBI, Homeland Security. I'll cover both under your original CLAVICLE finding. Far as anyone needs to know, this is still the same exfil."

Lynn relaxed. Lynn grateful.

Gary dropped onto her sofa. "You know, I trained with Michael."

Gary: jeans, desert boots, summer-weight linen sweater, shirtless beneath—Lynn noticed (not like she hadn't before)—Gary Gravin was the rare combination of intellect, relaxed cunning, sensitivity, style, and unavailability she found irresistible.

"He was head and shoulders above every one of us." He noticed her noticing him. Returned the look. With interest.

"Don't look at me that way, Gary. You're married."

"Don't I know it."

"The Chair of the Senate Select Committee? Believe me: everyone in the building knows it. A dozen years too old for you, by the way."

"Votes our way every time."

Their eyes touch. Hummingbird away. Zip-zap.

"At the Farm... no one trusted Michael." He returned to the subject at hand. "I didn't. Still don't—"

"Your mistake." She opened her bottom desk drawer.

Lynn poured two gins. Gary didn't react other than to take the mug. They both said, "Cheers." Casual. Accustomed.

He sipped. "We had a live-fire exercise. Two-man teams. Where you indemnify the Agency against accidental loss of life?"

Lynn knew it. Watched him drink. Left hers untouched. He saw. Unaccustomed. Didn't remark.

"I drew first choice." Gary swallowed gin. "Was glad. Meant no one else could pick Michael before me. Though he didn't care one way or the other, he's the reason I made it."

"Gary: if my brother's alive, he's gone off the reservation."

"So far, Michael's done nothing to lose the support of the Agency. Now he's coming home."

♛ ♛ ♛

THE DARK FIGURE OF A MAN dropped from the top of the Foxtail Farm automatic gate. Moved down the gravel drive to the main house. Front door unlocked, he slipped inside.

Outside. Night continued with cricket grind, frog chorus, horned owl backbeat in tall pines that stood wind-break sentinels along the road wall. A minute passed before Melody's scream braced Foxtail Farm into tense and frozen silence.

An upstairs window slammed open. Melody extended. Melody shouted: "Silas! Hal's home! My 'burglar's' home!"

Melody squealed, and Hal, mischief in his eyes, pulled her inside from behind. A moment after that, his balled fist knocked the window shut.

Crickets resume. Frogs up the volume. Owl takes off—*whooshes* the widow's walk that rings the four-sided, sloped roof of the North Vista Outhouse, where the black-iron carrion crow—bone in beak—turned when it wanted, regardless of the wind. Turned now. Where Silas Kingston paused in his work, turned as well to witness the events—the figure, the entry, the scream followed by his son pulling darling Melody into the bedroom, where Silas assumed they now made love.

He shut his eyes and whispered, "Thanks be to God."

Asked and answered with the return of the owl's call, Silas went back to rigging a long length of antenna wire along the horizontal of the black iron railing. Attached it to a concealed connector that ran a hidden coaxial to the weathervane.

ෞ෨෨

LYNN STOOD AT HER WINDOW. Stared at the section of Berlin Wall planted on CIA grounds. A Cold War gravestone. Her father's victory monument.

Rusty Aiken's, too. So many.

She thought of Russell Aiken too often when sober. And when she was drunk, she thought of Aiken more. Drunk/constant. But without any of the urgency real life demanded—so that was a plus for the cocktail column. Real life goaded. Real life made her question if she'd ever have the guts to break his heart.

Liar. It wouldn't break him, and that's what you're—

Lynn shuddered.

What you're wanting, right now, is right in that drawer—

She perked up at a sound outside her door.

How he'll appear. Someday.

Awaited a knock. Let herself pretend—just a harmless second—his unfeigned brown eyes, his crooked smile, and only a wall between them. No knock. Didn't see it until she'd almost stepped on it—the corner of an envelope poking beneath the door from the outer corridor. More than unusual; this was unheard of. Violation of regulations.

Someday. One day. This day?

She yanked the door wide. The brightly lit, long gray corridor: empty, both directions. Her hair rose on the back of her neck. A tingling sensation from her shoulders down her arms.

Lynn took the envelope. Recognized her brother's handwriting. "Sonuvabitch." She squeezed eyes, squeezed happy tears.

Returned to her desk. A dagger-style opener. Lynn slit the envelope. She peered inside before dumping the jigsaw photo pieces onto her desktop. The overhead white light had caught the sea glass wedged into the bottom corner. Lynn shook the envelope. The piece of glass bounced across her desktop. Fell to the carpet. She squeezed it between forefinger and thumb. Turned it under the light.

An unusual shade of blue. Of all the glass in her collection, she had only one similar piece. The piece at the bottom. The first piece.

3.

I T WOULD NEVER BE exactly like the first time, but it would always be the best time, every time; Hal and Melody, nude in one another's arms, their long legs warm and entwined, and Melody, as she always did afterward, massaging the sole of her foot on the hard knuckle of Hal's big toe. She said, "The boys asked if we could get a dog. Now we're in a house and all."

"I like it. Everything but the 'and all.'"

Melody gave a skeptical smile. "And that means what?"

"Means 'who.' Dad doesn't trust 'em."

"Dogs or boys?"

Before Hal could answer, glass shattered downstairs.

Seconds later. Boxers on. Pistol in fist. Hal passed beneath his mother, floating in her portrait. More alive than canvas makes possible. A mirror-army of himself in phalanx behind him, Hal found Silas on the porch. Whisk broom in hand. Broken crystal brandy snifter at his feet. The army dispersed as Hal crossed the threshold and joined his father.

Silas. "Hold. I'll sweep." Like they'd broken it together. He handed Hal a dustpan. "Then we drink."

Silas pulled a bottle of cognac, fresh snifters, from a cabinet.

"Michael's alive, Dad." He laid the dustpan of glass atop *The Once and Future King*.

"Never in doubt. Tell me."

"We had a hot extraction. The recovery team returned at daylight: no blood, no body. No sign of capture. Textbook escape and evasion."

Silas poured. One. The other. "And now, deference paid to need-to-know, National Security and non-disclosure rhetoric—all that law *not* in the Constitution—as family, start at the beginning. I will take every detail."

"As the man who taught me to hold sacred everything you deferred: accept I've told you all I will."

Because it was Hal, Silas accepted the rebuke.

"What are we drinking?" said Hal.

"A Hennessy cognac. *Timeless*."

"Any good?"

A wooden match. Heated crystal. One. The other. "Five K a bottle. Damn well better be."

Hal balked at the extravagance.

"It was a retirement gift." Silas slowly rolled one. Slowly, the other. Slowly on their sides—heat distributed. He put Hal's glass into Hal's hand. Raised the toast.

"To the Lord, for delivering my soldier son back to his family."

"To Michael... and whatever harebrained quest he's cooked up this time."

A moment of weakness; a side of Silas he would only ever show Hal. "Your brother—you don't think he's turned..."

"Not a chance."

♕ ♕ ♕

AFTER HAL caught the football.

Before cake. Before candle wishes.

Lynn walks with her mother along the sandy bank of the Patuxent River.

"It's important he hear how you feel from you, Linny."

"But when I say the wrong thing, Dad gets mad. Or laughs at me," she says, kicking sticks that railroad the shore. "Is it because I wasn't a boy, or's it I'm not girly enough?"

Doris stops. She takes both of Lynn's hands into her own. "Daddy loves you exactly as you are." Doris is sixteen years, four months, twelve days, eleven hours, forty-two minutes, twelve seconds, six heartbeats, and one breath away from eternity. "It's just— I believe, with the two of you— I think with him for *you—"*

Two false starts.

Two breaths.

Four heartbeats closer to dead.

"Lynn, I married Daddy because of the wonderful thing inside him missing in me; I knew with him I would be whole and happy. Silas married me—"

"Because of what was in you that's not in him?"

"Yes. Since you were born, both of us see perfectly within you: *not ourselves alone, but the thing we wished ourselves to be together, complete. Your father—the work he does, the world as* he *knows it—in the face of your perfection..."*

Doris can see her complicated explanation has lost Lynn... She also sees: the feelings behind her words have done their comfort.

"'If people reach perfection, they vanish, you know,'" Michael yelled back from where he's wandered ahead. "That's from your favorite book, Mom, huh?"

"In that story, King Arthur was talking about perfection as meeting God."

She doesn't expect either child to grasp the importance of that. She hardly cares. They're happy now, and she believes, mistakenly, she has time.

Michael, anxious to cheer up his sister, offers Lynn a piece of smooth, bluish beach glass. Lynn turns it over in her hand. Silky. Frosted white from sand abrasion.

"I thought you'd want it," he says.

Lynn spits in her hand. Moistens the glass. It glows. Bright robin's egg blue.

"You can add it to your collection."

"It's not a real collection."

"Make it one." Michael grins.

Lynn looks at her brother. All stretched lips and teeth. Knows he's trying to make up for not defending her against their father as he would want to were he yet a man. "It's pretty. This'll be the official first piece. Okay? I'll save all the best ones from now on. You and Mom and Hal can help me find them."

Doris says: "What makes the best ones best?"

Lynn says: "Magic. Magic memories."

The wind whips her auburn hair across her face as Lynn turns to the sun. Lynn tilts her chin. Lynn holds the piece of beach glass to the sun to dazzle her eyes. Magic. Memory. Memory magic.

Far away, a telephone rings. Not magic. Lynn hates it. Pretends it doesn't ring, and she cannot hear it ring—

The magic. The memories. Memories lived backwards to Russell Aiken coming to claim her and the gift she has prepared for him all these years...

—and something else that needs to be said.

Ring, ring, ring...

What? What? Where is it?

The memory emerges. Where she's buried it on the shore. Where she's buried all her other memories. Her frightful memories.

The wind hums through the beach grass.

"It's like inside my kaleid—"

"Lynn! Careful!" Doris checks her tone. "Careful. Broken glass cuts worst of all."

Michael gives his sister a pointed look. A loud look that says more than a voice: You almost said it. You almost said the word.

What the heck does that mean?

Michael? Mom?

(Silas, don't ask such a terrible thing.)

Ring-a-ding-ding.

Russell. Rusty.

Lynn drops the broken glass in the front pocket of her sleeveless denim shirt. She holds out her arms and spins, and the sun in the sky and off the water, beaming through the branches of the trees, spellbinds her and dizzies.

✡ ✡ ✡

PIECES OF PHOTOGRAPHS lay in disarray, Lynn, asleep. Head on her desk. Gin mug untouched at her elbow. The secure phone: *Ring... Ring... Ring*. Lynn stared at the glass cylinder of beach glass.

"Kaleidoscope."

Lynn ignored the telephone. One moment more.

The river wide; the river cool. Insistent. She listens. The wind moans over the treetops.

Cool: white sheets—the one time with Aiken.

And the rest of her life.

Given away. Because sisters save brothers, and brothers save sisters. And the children are the lambs we lead; the flock we shield from the wolves. Oh, Michael. Don't do this. Your candle was "Loyalty."

She made a sigh. Put sound to it for measure. To expel her thoughts as static. She arranged the pieces of cut photographs into a kaleidoscopic circle.

Lynn saw the pattern.

"Hello?" Into the receiver.

Her free hand sorted image combinations.

"Arrival pushed to twenty hundred hours." Male voice. Other end of the call. Lead officer/recovery team. Posed travelers/Dulles International.

"Why the delay?"

"Deplaned in Frankfurt. Switched to a later flight."

Lynn frowned. Lynn placed the last triangles. Picasso had nothing on Michael. As old-school as Michael's method was, what he'd given his sister was as good as the best computer biometric algorithm. A man of many faces. Same man. This man, like all men: possessed a singular symmetry—brow to lips, eye to eye, iris to earholes, mouth to jaw line, nose to lips, nose to ears—essence no man ever perfectly disguised.

A placeholder in her mind. And a word.

Broken glass cuts worst of all.

Lynn dubbed Michael's subject *Kaleidoscope.* Had no idea, but for her internal pronunciation, she was already one hundred percent correct.

👑👑👑

As REQUIRED: Lynn completed the requisition form in triplicate. Referenced: KALEIDOSCOPE. Referenced: CLAVICLE. Signed. Handed across the counter to "Burlington"—an imaginary codename spun from her interior monologue for the middle-aged duty officer who, for as long as Lynn remembered, ran the desk for the Central Asia Active-Operational File Library. Nicknamed due to his habit of wearing a Burlington Coat Factory sweater every day of every year. Lynn couldn't remember ever seeing him wear the same sweater twice.

"I'll be taking these back to my office."

"Yes, Ms. Kingston."

He laid the form on the counter to log Lynn's request into his terminal. His face was pale. Lips, always a tad too moist, saliva always stringing between them. His skin was thin. Translucent. The way Lynn imagined moth larvae. Probably the reason she'd never seen him in the same sweater twice. He ate them. Burlington's expression tightened.

"Ma'am, you're not cleared for KALEIDOSCOPE product."

KALEIDOSCOPE: existence confirmed.

"Not entirely, of course..." Lynn indicated a line on the requisition, subtly slipping the form back toward herself. Pinned it with her index finger. "Only interested in my CLAVICLE product."

His fingers clattered keys. "Ma'am: you're not cleared for CLAVICLE product, either."

What the fuck?

Lynn slid the form closer.

"Ms. Kingston. I will need that requisition."

He attempted to take it. Lynn snatched it from the counter.

"CLAVICLE is mine. My officer, my agent, my operation."

"The requisition, please."

Lynn pocketed it. Went to the door.

"How many years you got here—" she recalled his real name, infantilizing it into— "Freddy?"

"Nearing nineteen, Ms. Kingston. Now, please, the—"

"You know, Freddy-boy? Kingstons have over three-quarters of a century. My dad—you remember Silas, ex-Chief of Counterintelligence—that bastard used to say, 'Makes everyone else in this drafty old castle come off as a guest.' Button up, kiddo."

The duty officer waited until Lynn was gone—door closed behind her/full five seconds—before he turned. Burlington's tongue tickled his lips. From within, Associate Deputy Director Counterintelligence Morton Drexler stepped forward.

Sunday, July Fourth - Independence Day

1.

H AL TILTED, SHOULDER NUDGING the door frame of his childhood bedroom. Melody had chosen this room for the twins, and the twins liked it for the shelf of their father's trophies that commemorated his accomplishments. From YMCA Indian Guides Pinewood Derby race cars and their colored ribbons to junior high and high school sports medals and team cups; Annapolis citations, Basic Training, then Marine Corps, then Recon: patches, ribbons, decorations. All the regalia never worn once operating black. The twins called it "Daddy's Treasure Room."

Hal smoked English tobacco from one of his father's Dunhill's. As the smoke drifted in, Melody spun on her knee, threw open a window, and said—a sewing needle clinched between lips— "I don't mind your holiday smoking. I really don't. But couldn't you wait until we made it outside?" She pivoted back to their sons. Proceeded to finish their costumes, fingers deft with needle, thread, scissor-snips, and long-ago skills.

Jack was Daniel Boone, complete with coonskin cap, a "buckskin" vest made from an attic sofa cushion; Little Silas: An American Indian with wild turkey feathers and "buckskin" britches made from the same sofa's back panel.

"Honey," said Melody, applying face paint to Little Silas's cheeks—red stripe, white stripe, blue— "I adore your father." Hal puffed smoke signals from the briar. "For Silas to come up with this spur-of-the moment Patriotic Review..." She *mmm'd* appreciation.

"Actually, we used to do 'em. The tradition goes back at Foxtail to when dad was a kid. Probably even further. Ready boys?"

"Daddy," Jack pronounced as if what he'd say next was irrefutable. "We need a dog."

"Didn't Daniel Boone have goldfish? Honey?"

Melody tossed a playful frown. Gathered stray thread. "Maybe one day, boys."

👑 👑 👑

FLOOR-AND-A-HALF BELOW. Main stairway landing. Gwen and Michael's three daughters faced the large and tilted American Federal mirror Silas hung on the side wall once upon a time, before any of them were born. Sideways to the portrait of their grandmother, whom Paige and Charlotte had met alive but only remembered fogged and vague. Leigh, not at all. They made final adjustments to the character costumes each would model in the parade across the yard. From the close side-angle, looming above, Doris appeared less eager to step from the canvas than she did from the dead-on view. From this angle, the lilies in her grip looked like a green paper cone launching red blooms of pyrotechnic fire. Already anticipating/participating in the living holiday.

All three girls were used to the illusions Papa's mirrors reflected. As if every glass offered its own interpretation of their grandmother. Paige and Charlotte spent many hours of many days—varying light/varying weather—moving room to room, varying their own mirror-facing angles, playing with this magic. Had grown to know more about Doris in reflection than in photo albums, reminiscences, than in all the *then* before-and-after the memories had covered with dust.

With falling ash.

They two older girls had developed a code for the different qualities presented by different looking glasses.

CCD=Come Closer Doris

GAD=Go Away Doris

AD=Angry Doris

SD=Sad Doris

HD=Happy Doris

DFWD=Don't Fuck With Doris

And—giggle—XED=Sexy Doris

No matter her mood, they were always glad for and felt caressed by her company.

Dressed as American patriot Nathan Hale, Paige tied a length of clothesline rope in a hangman's knot. Charlotte and Leigh portrayed, in turn, the Statue of Liberty—bedsheet toga, aluminum foil crown, and torch—and Paul Revere in clamdigger britches with a basement-rescued hobby horse. Threadbare, velveteen head; a missing-button eye.

From above, Melody led the twins, passing with, "You guys look great. Good for you!"

Hal carried the rear; a caboose chuffing stove-smoke from his pipe-stack.

"Welcome home, Uncle Hal," said Paige, knowing each time he returned meant he'd made others safe and would now keep them that way too.

"Hi, Uncle Hal," said Charlotte, distracted by the empty white gift box disguised to make her tablet.

"I heard you come home!" Leigh singsonged. "You and Aunt Melody sounded like you had a tickle war."

Paige and Charlotte exchanged grins to see their warrior uncle hustle by—cheeks burning hotter than his tobacco.

♛ ♛ ♛

MELODY AND GWEN stood with Silas on the wide steps where Doris once experienced a premonition of doom replace joy on her birthday. They waited as Hal organized the children to pass in review.

"Silas, why don't you like dogs?" Melody.

"Ever seen what happens when a dog discovers its reflection in a mirror?" Silas.

"I'm more a 'go-fetch' dog person." Melody.

"And that's fine, until old 'fetch' looks in a mirror and he suddenly sees God. Ruined many a family."

Standing behind Melody, Gwen rolled her eyes.

"The boys are hoping for an outside dog."

Silas looked away. "Here they come. Let's pay attention."

Gwen smirked. *Aww. Poor sis'.*

Hal led the twins past, both boys *woo-woo-wooing*, open palms bouncing off O-shaped mouths.

"An outside dog is the only kind I will allow."

The Silas stamp of approval?!

Gwen held her tongue—clamped between her teeth. Silas led the two women in a round of applause for the boys. Melody ringed her fingers and whistled.

Leigh came next, astride her horse-head stick, prancing past. Stopped beside the twins. Flung her hair. Faced the house. "'Listen my children and you shall hear...the midnight ride of Paul Revere'—I can't remember any more!"

Charlotte bustled beside her. Braced at attention. Torch uplifted. "'Bring me your tired, your poor, your huddled masses yearning to breathe free!'"

Paige. Last up. Cheerful. Good-sporting it because, after all, she was almost eighteen: "I only regret that I have one life to lose for my country." Laughing. She pulled the dangling end of the clothesline rope into the air. Stuck out her tongue—*I-do-what-I-want*— "Ugh!"

The inappropriateness of her prank shone clear on the faces of the adults.

Teen desperation. "I didn't mean anything by it."

Gwen flashed an extra-dirty look.

Melody offered sympathy on a wilted smile.

Silas looked at his lambs. Except for Paige. He stepped off the porch. Approached the line of children. Comported himself a field marshal.

Jack offered a goofy smile. The kind a child wears when he senses something wrong but has no idea what; only that it couldn't possibly be something he did...unless he had done it.

"Jack: when I look at you, I remember the Cumberland Gap and American expansion."

The boy twisted his mouth. Smiled till it hurt. No idea what Papa meant. Except he wasn't in trouble. *Phew.*

"Little Silas." Silas stepped to the next boy. Hard look at his face. His warpaint. "Hmm. If we had any tea, we would go, you and I, to Boston Harbor and hurl it in."

He addressed Charlotte. "Charlotte, you rise tall; a beautiful reminder the French aren't utterly unredeemable. Know this: for generations, Kingstons have given blood in honor of that torch. That stone-carved Declaration of Independence. That liberty crown."

Melody's fingers found Gwen's as Silas indicated the foil beams of light haloing the girl's head.

"May I keep this?" Silas said.

Charlotte lifted the tinfoil crown from her head. Presented it to him with an impromptu dip of her knee. He lowered his head. She rested the crown lightly upon it.

He moved on. "Leigh: the consummate Paul Revere." He circled the child. "I especially appreciate your choice of Longfellow. I look forward to you reciting all thirteen stanzas. When you do—" he produced a fifty-dollar bill from where it had been tucked inside his palm the whole time. He tore it down the middle. Gave Leigh half.

"I win?" Leigh smiled, eyes dancing to the other children, her mother, back to Silas. Silas brandished the other half in front of her eager face.

"I will show you a trick to reconstruct this, and when we deposit it on September third, the bank will never know it was torn."

"Thank you, Papa... Wait! That's Daddy's birthday!"

"Correct. It is also the date on which King George surrendered and thirteen colonies became the United States of America. We grabbed the stick that spins the globe. Well done."

Through all of this, Paige's concern she'd done the unconscionable increased. Silas stepped before her. He circled Paige.

"I'm not sure where you found that rope."

"I'm—"

"Or learned a hangman's knot."

"Papa, I wasn't thinking of Daddy—"

"Yale University has a statue of Nathan Hale. Did you know that?"

He inspected her from behind. Eyes up. Eyes down. Her spine straight. His gaze extra dramatic, even though Paige could not see it.

Paige: eyes front, soldier on parade ground. "No, Papa!"

"Of course, there is no rope around that neck. Nor is it symbolic of why Nathan Hale is an American hero. He looks like a fancy pants fool." He changed direction. Another orbit. "In the garden outside my old office, there is a different statue. Hale at his most heroic. Rope round his neck. Ready to hang. Spitting it back in the Redcoats' faces. Recite it for me, Paige, but do it like my Nathan Hale did: defiant to the end."

"I only regret that I have one life—"

"That's the Yale-Hale." Silas punched air. "Mean it!"

"I only regret that I have one life to lose for my country!"

"Again!"

So, Paige did, overcome by the defiance Silas implored her to, defiance like her father felt in those last moments before he vanished. The defiance that fueled Michael now, because no one vanishes—not really—and Silas lifted both his arms like a conductor, or a Moses, or best a Merlyn, and her sisters joined Paige, and it felt fiery, and felt good. It felt right. Kingston. Felt American.

Hal had moved onto the steps. He admired the emotion in Melody's eyes. He loved his wife. Pressed his lips to her cheek.

Gwen leaned over. "The old coot always gets the elephant in the room to dance with him," as if that were a bad thing.

Melody blinked a tear from her eye. Smiled to disguise the thing she cried over. Because that thing—the thing that had set her on her mission to become a Kingston—was a thing meant to destroy all of this and all of them.

The tradition goes back at Foxtail to when dad was a kid. Probably even farther.

A horrible thing. Stalking thing. Coming thing. And sooner than she was prepared for: a thing menacing and evil that would present itself at the Kingston gates.

If I can become a Kingston, can't "farther" become too far and held back by grace?

Hal noticed Melody brush away the tear. "You okay?"

Melody: "I'm so happy with our life."

Silas checked his watch. "All right, Paige. Get what you need. If you follow instructions, make good time on the road, and if we move fast once we get there, we'll be back before two."

"I'm driving somewhere?"

"It's only just nine." Gwen said, confused. "Where could you be going that would take that long?"

Silas took Paige's hand. Slapped his Cadillac keys into her open palm.

Gwen whined. "She doesn't know how to drive! I've never really taken her!"

Paige beamed.

"She'll be a better driver than you when we get back."

Gwen shifted foot-to-foot like the vexed bird that knows a stick can't move.

Baffled, Melody looked to Hal for clarity. His easy smile matched Paige's. "She won the review."

"Leigh won!" Gwen protested. The stick was a snake.

"The money prize is second place." Hal moved from the porch to gather their sons. They bolted with war whoops for the overgrown tobacco fields.

👑 👑 👑

OFF THE 83, ACROSS THE MARYLAND BORDER just inside Pennsylvania, if you know where to find it and Silas surely did, a massive concrete bunker sits within two acres clear-cut from the deep and surrounding forest. Paige navigated Silas's sapphire-black, 1992 Cadillac Brougham into the asphalt parking lot. She'd once docked Morgan's father's Sea Ray—not particularly well but hadn't crashed into the pier or anything—yet this vehicle was more in line with an aircraft carrier than a cabin cruiser.

"This oughta be fun," she said, and joined the flow of vehicles weaving the lanes, avoiding shoppers pushing overloaded carts like ammo teams on a Civil War battlefield.

"Do I circle until I find someone leaving?"

"That is the usual method. Are you confident you can park in one of these spaces?"

Not on your f-ing life, Pops.

"Like yea-ah... What? You think I'm nervous?" She made a *pshh* sound with her lips.

"Paige, this vehicle is eighteen feet long."

"B. F. D."

Silas studied his granddaughter. Appreciated her bluster.

"If I slow down, I can wait for these guys. They look like they're going to that SUV up there." She gave him a sly sidelong glance and lifted her foot from the gas pedal.

"You'd do it? You're prepared to turn into that narrow space and park?"

"You gave me the keys."

A crew of fraternity boys in Greek-letter sweatshirts. One of them noticed Paige. Liked what he saw. Pointed at her. Pointed at his SUV. She tapped the tip of her nose—liked it all right back—bingo. He gave her a thumbs-up and a wink.

Quite enough for Silas. "You'll park in the red at the front."

"The fire lane?" She waved at the boys.

'Bye, guys.

The young men chased her with whistles.

"It says they'll ticket and tow."

"Not when they run these plates. Do it."

Paige made a wide turn at the end of the lane. Glided alongside the curb. "And if there's a fire?"

Silas gave her a dumb stare. Shifted his glance. Her eyes followed. The sign above the double glass doors.

Red, White, and BOOM! Fireworks.

She put the car in park. "Oh. We're all dead anyway."

"Thata girl. Let's go."

👑 👑 👑

CROWNED WITH CHARLOTTE'S TINFOIL, Silas pushed the cart. Paige filled it: from sparklers to three-foot rockets, from ground batteries to tube-launched shells.

"Papa, we'll never shoot all this off."

"You'd be surprised. Get some of those 'Gibbering Idiots.'" Silas enjoyed renaming each item to his fancy. "Mmmm. 'Blind the Sighted' and 'Cure the Deaf,' always liked both of those." Extra-loud. Extra-sneering. To provoke other customers around them. "What-ho? 'Causes for Insanity in Cats.' Ingenious. And a 'Torment the Grumpy Neighbor—' Two of them, please. Isn't this place great?"

"You're funny," Paige said, and grabbed them all. Laughed with Silas until they wheeled into the check-out line.

There was a mother. In front of them. Too stout for her t-shirt. Don't ask about her jean shorts. A pair of lumpy children inside her cart. Mother turned up her nose. Made a snit-snivel noise.

Silas nodded at her kids. "Seemed to have missed those. Which aisle?"

"Sir, have you ever considered that the behavior of elders becomes that of their offspring?"

"My, you're sassy."

"I am serious. Sir."

Silas reappraised her. "That is something I consider constantly, madame. Which is why my every word contains a lesson important to their upbringing as Kingstons and Americans. Surely, you have loved ones who've patriotically served?"

Ding! Paige's phone went off inside her purse.

The woman didn't answer Silas, but her expression appeared to say, *Go on*, which Silas would have done in any case.

"In the heat of battle, since America's founding—"

Paige retrieved her device; the notification screen was blank.

"—American patriots have written on their ordnance. Humorous slogans. Comedy in the face of battle. Some of it obscene. But faced with the threat of ultimate sacrifice, true Americans..."

As Silas continued his history lesson, Paige dug deeper into her purse. She found—surreptitiously checked—the phone given her two nights before.

A WhatsApp message: *I'M OUTSIDE. I HAVE TO SEE YOU.*

Paige hesitated. Finger poised over the keypad. Knows the answer to her question before she keys: *MORGAN?*

Ding! CLIVE.

"At Gettysburg—you boy's been there yet? Seen the Cyclorama? Walked Pickett's Charge abreast of twelve-thousand phantoms?"

Paige waggled the phone at Silas. "Morgan. She wants to know what we're doing tonight. May I take it?"

👑 👑 👑

THE SILVER RENTAL FORD and Paige's hella hot rescuer from beach embarrassment—

That's all it was. All Deeb ever can be. Embarrassment.

—was easy to locate. She approached his open window.

"You do know what a creeper you are, following me two hours? Here. Take it."

He didn't take the phone. "I want you to keep it. Maybe I could talk to you after I'm gone."

"College trip for the summer?"

"I work in government. British government."

Paige tried hard not to appear thrown. Played a goofy smirk. "Brits investigating my family?"

Time to walk. But the secret of this young British spy: too tempting to a daughter of spies.

"Don't worry. It's just—people like him—your grandad—retired from high-level jobs in national security where a question lingers among allies—"

"Silas Kingston's a patriot. It's Clive, right? Clive what?"

"Lancer." Their eyes met. Paige dropped her gaze. "On another July Fourth, your best patriots were Great Britain's worst enemies."

"On this Fourth, you're an asshole. Clive Lancer."

She flipped him the phone. He caught it—one hand. Caught her wrist—the other.

"Whole thing's rubbish. Agreed. It's just—Hot wars end with a bang. Cold Wars...? Questions linger. Even among the cousins. Routine vetting, a must-do. Every few years. I could go to prison for telling you this—"

"Do. I can't be talking to you."

He released her. "Your grandad cleared."

"I gotta go." But Paige didn't move.

"He always clears. Why British Intelligence assigns Silas Kingston to the lowest geezer on the Allied Espionage ladder—because it never amounts to a thing."

He turned his head, peered out the windshield. He remained looking off when he said, "Paige: I came this summer to spy on Silas Kingston. Instead... I want to see you."

"You don't know me."

"I know everything about you. I know you prefer Rascal Flatts while your friends prefer Rhianna—"

"I love Ree-Ree."

"But you listen to Country when you're alone. You love animals. You once had a flying squirrel—"

"Sugar glider."

"You hate tomatoes—"

"Uh, did you say, 'tom*ah*toes? Doof.'"

"—but you love pizza. You eavesdrop on your mother's phone calls. And you are your father's biggest defender."

Clive's eyes shifted to the storefront. Paige followed his gaze. Silas exited the store in friendly conversation with the sassy mother and her children. He held two receipts. The mother was trying to write Silas a check. He refused.

"I really gotta go. Keep your phone, Clive Lancer. You've seriously weirded me out."

"Weird would be me not admitting I fancy you." He put his phone back in her hand. He closed her fingers around it. She let him.

Clive grinned. Hopeful. Movie star eyes. Paige put the phone in her pocket.

When Silas arrived at his Cadillac, Paige was waiting alone to be piped aboard.

2.

C HARLOTTE AND LEIGH DRAPED bunting. They coiled streamers around and all along the porch railing. Paige followed the twins, her arms filled with the miniature American flags she handed them. They planted flags along the edges of the stairs. They planted flags along flowerbed borders. They planted flags in every particular or peculiar place they hankered to poke a hole, and Paige enjoyed them enjoying themselves, and she didn't fixate on Clive movie-star-spy Lancer, not more than a quick one thousand times. And another one hundred again. Just for fun. Just to feel her heart crack a smile at the thought, *Clive Lancer*.

Gwen watched Melody set the white-washed picnic table for the evening's barbeque.

Hal prepared the split-barrel smoker, pouring chunks of mesquite charcoal. Ash dust billowed. Hal coughed.

Melody looked to Hal. Swiveled her head all around. "Where's Silas?"

"Down to the Outhouse cellar for wine."

Table set: Melody rubbed her hands together with satisfaction. "Might as well lend him a hand."

Ah-ah-ah. He doesn't like anyone down there.

"You do that." Gwen sat back. Fanned herself with a napkin Melody had just folded. "And find us something afternoony-sweet. Something light. Ah, hell—might as well do us one of each."

SILAS MOVED THROUGH COBWEBBED SPACES between dusty shelves of cased wine and single, dusty bottles. Stopped at an empty crate. Beneath the straw at the bottom, he retrieved two framing nails, points bent into hooks.

End of the next row. Silas crouched. Nails inserted into wall holes. Silas gave a twist. A practiced pull. Opened a false panel—size of a playhouse door. Withdrew a grimy box. Opened a flap. A small and scuffed leather-bound book lay on top of an old radio transceiver.

"Silas?" Melody called. Came cautious down dim, unimproved wooden stairs. Stepped inside the stone-cool, straw/wood/dust-scented room. Peered down aisles. No sign of— "Silas?"

"Just in time." Right at her shoulder.

She spun. The box he carried was closed. Two dingy bottles of wine, wobbled loose atop its lid.

"Take these before they fall. I'll grab a few more from inside this—" he hefted the radio box— "and follow right up."

Behind her father-in-law, the secret panel stood ajar. Melody noticed. Didn't remark. Silas noticed that. Melody gave him a sunny smile. A smile he would one day take with him to his grave.

✤✤✤

AT THE FAR EDGE OF THE LAWN, abutting the top of the rickety beach stairs, Hal worked a heavy spade in sandy soil. Dug a trench. His rippling muscles mesmerized the children. Awed by the Recon Marine tattoo that crossed the length of his upper chest. Extended as artistic plate armor over his right shoulder blade like a knight's sleeve depicting the skull-and-crossed oars on the red spear-point of his battalion's insignia. Inked as though in bolted steel.

"So cool," Jack said, and Little Silas grinned and nodded.

"Hal!" Lynn shouted from afar.

Hal tossed his shovel. Climbed from the trench. Lynn ran to him across the lawn. The fatigue of having slept at her desk faded to the power of her younger brother's sculpted arms.

✤✤✤

RAGGED-EDGED T-BONES and gnawed drumsticks, beef and pork rib shafts stacked on greasy plates as if for carting to the ossuary. Gwen and Melody lingered over tin-tasting strawberry shortcake. Elbows perched between bottles. Wine and root beer. Ginger beer. Bottles standing. Bottles fallen. Empty and enjoyed. Silas shouted battle cries. Led the girls in a reckless Roman candle charge against Hal who—crazy to be smoking his hand-me-down pipe while playing with gunpowder—blocked exploding fireballs with a trash can lid. Fired back his own. The girls dodged. They laughed. Silas batted flaming missiles with open palms causing them to explode like case shells overhead. Lynn crouched with a lighter. Lit fresh sparklers for the twins—one after the other as each spark-fizzing stick burned down and was discarded in a tendril puff of vanishing smoke.

On the North Vista Outhouse porch steps, Paige sat apart spinning the football, catching it, dreaming about Clive Lancer.

Sad and beautiful darkness came to Foxtail Farm. "Sad and beautiful darkness"—where did I get that...?

"The glorious thing about him was his eye... This sad and beautiful darkness." White's unicorn.

The man come to spy on Papa—spin football/catch football—but whose noble eyes had fallen like raining comets upon her head. Her heart.

What's so important about the past, anyway?

She floated above it all and somehow didn't remember: when the unicorn came to the virgin, and when the brothers came to the unicorn, they slaughtered it without mercy.

👑👑👑

"WE SHOULD FIND SOMEONE for Lynn." Melody sipped coffee from a Styro-cup.

"Huh?" Gwen sounded. "We've never been through this?" Although they were directly across the picnic table from each other, Gwen peered at Melody as though from across unbreakable railroad tracks.

"Through what?"

"Hun, Lynn had someone. Carl Sumpthin—worked the Smithsonian Castle. She wasn't a lush, then." Tipsy/sour/Gwen.

Melody upended the corners of her mouth to mask a frown.

Was there ever a pot smaller than a kettle?

"You know how it is," Gwen slur-snarled. "'Cause he wasn't Agency, Lynn had a cover story while they dated."

"This Carl— He wasn't the one who..."

"No."

👑👑👑

A BREAK IN THE BATTLE. The twins having cajoled their cousins to teach them to write their names in the air with their bamboo sticks of colored sparks, Hal took a minute to grab two beers from a trash can-turned-cooler. The corner of the broad lawn. He cracked the cap on the first. Offered the bottle to Lynn, who leaned against a large field stone. A tall rainbird, bolted to the rock, created in twilight the silhouette of a rising sword.

"Cold one?"

"Quit."

"Quit beer?"

"Quit-quit."

"You've said that before."

"For good this time. Can't say 'forever,' but for 'good.' Need to get out of my fog to see through the fog around me."

Hal chuckled. "'Clear-eyed and unassailable?'"

"Dusting off my stock phrase for me, huh?" She didn't share his laugh.

Hal couldn't pretend to know what Lynn was after this time, but she was his sister and a Kingston, so he knew Lynn did. All Hal needed. Simple that way. A what's-at-the-end-of your-gunsight kind of guy.

♛ ♛ ♛

GWEN COMBINED THE DREGS of three bottles into her cup. "Agency vetted him. Ol' Carl came up clean as soap. Lynn got permission to marry the guy. So, she got him to propose."

"Oh, no."

"Betcher boots, kid. Jus' like you. Jus' like me— 'And with this ring' came the truth about the job and this family." Gwen swallowed her crap mélange. "It's hard for anyone to love crazy."

"Crazy?"

"Especially if you're an outsider."

"Who's crazy?"

"Hun, Silas is a loon, and my husband Michael ain't far off."

"But if he loved Lynn—I mean, finding out about the Company made me love Hal that much more."

"Lookit, let's agree: there's some can take the life, some who can't."

Melody came to her feet. She wouldn't believe Gwen. Rejected Gwen's words. She loved this family, her family, the goodness she found in each of them.

We share one light—even you, Gwen.

She looked around.

My family. Here. That's the only *thing waiting for me.* This *is what is mine.*

And Melody knew in that instant. How small and childish she felt because she'd known all along. After the crime—awful/foolish. Before the promise—foolish/awful. Before Hal. Before Silas became a *real* father. She would discover the thing that had brought her here—the promise; the *oath*—but she wouldn't let anyone, not even flesh and blood, betray her Kingstons.

With this ring: I am Kingston.

At the fireworks pit, Hal and Paige began the nation's celebration with a flight of skyrockets. Silver. Gold. Flash, sparkle, *boom, bam, boom,* jeweled fire—orange and purple—rain.

♛ ♛ ♛

LYNN WALKED to her car. Her cellphone jangled. She answered. The voice of her superior. "Lynn? Gary. You at Dulles yet?"

"Nervous for me? This isn't my first fireworks show."

"It's about something earlier. Something to do with a requisition form?"

Lynn *beeped* open her Porsche's locks. "So what? I changed my mind about something. Big deal. Tell Freddy to get a helmet. Why're you calling?"

She could hear distance-softened explosions in his background. She pictured the symmetry of his face bathed in flashes of colored light.

"You're right. It's not a big deal." Lynn slowly seated herself inside her car. "Be careful tonight. Lynn, if I lost you..."

Lynn's blood paused in her veins.

Maybe it was the heat of the night, maybe the rush of fireworks, maybe the cocktails she knew he'd be drinking, maybe it was all three, but he spoke almost freely when he said, "Say something meaningful. For both of us."

The night was hot. She wasn't drinking. It was suspicion. It was also hope. And all of them combined in a surge of blood. She buried emotion. Went operational. "What's Kaleidoscope?"

The sudden space between them became like the sunlight-poisoning void between Headquarters' windowpanes.

♛♛♛

ABOVE ALL ELSE, Gary Gravin knew he should disconnect. His wife, Senator Theresa Ossani, watched him from a cluster of party guests. This was Director Jeremy Harker's annual—for the past three years since his presidential appointment and cock-a-hoop return to Langley—Seventh Floor soiree. Theresa's mesmerizing gold-flecked gray eyes, the source of lifelong compliments, blazed with jealousy.

Gary whispered into his device. "It's older than the Agency. Mostly 'Director's Eyes Only.'"

"Mostly?"

"I wouldn't be sure Harker's cleared."

"And *you?*"

"On its face, Kaleidoscope is about worldwide energy. Resources. Procurement. Stockpile. The 'why-eternal' of all conflict—so they say. But Lynn: I'm not cleared for anything more than the headline and the warning I receive whenever Ops accidentally bumps up against it. *You* don't go there. Drexler's gun-dogging you as it is." His eyes found Drexler on the edge of a group of sycophants—CIA courtiers of all sorts. The fantasists, jesters, Intelligence Community intriguers, easy money overlords, arms-laundering foreign nobility—unified by imperial capital greed.

"It's what Michael came onto in Turkey, isn't it?"

"Drop Turkey. A correction is being made. Forget it. Michael's almost home."

Lynn fell silent. But the line remained connected. She replied: flat tone, flat-line, flat heart— "Call you from the airport when I have him."

Manicured hands squeezed the DDO's shoulders. Massaged them. Gary disconnected his phone. Turned into his wife's sinuous, perfumed arms. "I was missing you, Resa," he told her the lie she needed to hear. Always.

Musicians played a big band foxtrot. Harker and his wife were fabulous dancers. Owned Arthur Murry franchises. And all the others joined them on the outdoor floor.

Between the hard edge thirty years in the Senate had chiseled into Theresa, and Gary's remarkable glow of youth that nothing could dim, in the illusory lights of this holiday night, they might have been mistaken for an unseemly mother and her son.

"I make one demand, Gary. You dance only with me."

3.

THE CANADIAN PASSPORT WITH Michael Kingston's photograph was a perfect CIA forgery. It bore the name *Arthur Danford*. Were it to be put to detailed scrutiny by Customs Border Protection, it would backstop against a valid Ontario driver's license. Backstop active bank accounts. Backstop a robust online presence with heavily populated Facebook, Twitter, and Instagram threads. A home address current in its water, power, and gas utilities—backstopped by varied and consistent usage. Arthur Danford claimed an active library card as well and—if anyone investigated—enjoyed mysteries, and cookbooks, and histories of the knights of the Norman Conquest, Gauls, and the Saxons.

Michael's sister, posing as a businesswoman, waited in baggage claim. She checked her smartphone screen. It displayed Michael's false passport information. She watched the Passport Control computer approve his entry in real-time. And the CBP officer who checked the passport, who eyeballed Michael's photograph against the individual presenting it, passed Arthur/Michael through his checkpoint.

Lynn placed the device against her cheek. When she spoke at it, her voice was picked up by the earwig radio transceiver hidden in her ear.

"Stand by to move." Lynn worked her way to meet the flow of travelers released from Michael's flight from Frankfurt. "Move to intercept."

Her lead officer and his partner moved from left and right flanks. Into the crowd flow. Headed toward the Frankfurt flight's baggage carousel.

Lynn caught sight of her brother's head. His shoulders. The collar of the jacket she bought him last Christmas.

"Can you see his face?" Lynn stepped forward, only to be blocked by two elderly women. They argued over a knitting bag.

Similar human blocks stalled her two officers. They used heavy hands to pass.

A pair of uniformed TSA Federal Air Marshals bracketed "Arthur Danford." Hustled him to the far side of an empty baggage carousel.

Lynn's eyes focused on Michael struggling against his captors. Lynn shoved between the two gray-haired women.

Silver flickered, catching light.

An open pair of 6-inch Chinese scissors pierced her neck.

Lynn's hands flew to the blood-streaming wound. Her horror doubled as she helplessly watched a silenced pistol shoved into the base of her brother's skull. Her blood flowed. Her knees buckled.

Trigger pull—*Pffpt!* A red balloon of blood blown from Michael's head.

The TSA assassins dropped the corpse onto the baggage carousel, which pulled it through the rubber-flapped exit.

Travelers screamed at the carnage. Panic rippled from the pair of deadly events. Her vision fading, Lynn observed the pair of TSA killers run. Her lead officer hit his knees and slid to her side. His partner followed Michael's body into the baggage loading bay.

Pandemonium engulfed the airport. Alarms blared. Airport police and SWAT flooded the scene.

The TSA assassins rushed to a specific and unmarked door. Keycard ready. The first swiped the lock. The light remained red. They shared a brief glance. The first raked the key again.

And again.

"Drop your weapon!"

And again. The second assassin spun with his suppressed pistol. A short burst of gunfire from the trio of SWAT officers.

The pair went down.

The special operators trained their weapons on the bodies, leaving nothing to chance. Did a strange thing. A swipe of one of their own cards. They stepped over the dead and disappeared through the unmarked door.

♛ ♛ ♛

BLEEDING OUT, Lynn's blood flowed through her hair and across the floor. She fought against unconsciousness, her sight dimming on her lead officer applying pressure to her neck, her throat—

Stay awake.

Stay alive.

This isn't dying. Stay awake.

A pair of EMTs. Orange plastic boxes slammed against the floor.

Sounds far away. Don't let it get farther. Clear-eyed/unassailable. Don't. Let. It. Go.

Michael climbs the neighbors' wall. "No one ever picks them. They'll just go to waste. C'mon." He reaches back for her, fingers grasping.

"They're not our oranges."

Plasma bag. Surgical glue. They worked against her ebbing life.

👑👑👑

THERE IS A MARVELOUS VIEW of the Patuxent from the iron walkway of the North Vista Outhouse. Here, Silas watched the skyrockets. The firework shells his son and nieces launched over the river. While he despised himself, Silas Kingston loved his family. He would do anything to protect and keep them. He always had. He attached the antenna wire strung the night before to the two-way radio he'd pulled from its hiding place in the wine cellar.

Its dials, its back panel: Russian. Silas opened the codebook. Russian as well. He dialed into the appropriate frequency. Under bright and dazzling rockets' red glare—the Kingston celebration radiant—he lifted the hand-mike.

"Kalaydoskop, Kalaydoskop. Cat's Eye to Kalay-doskop..."

👑👑👑

A MOSCOW LISTENING POST. A junior FSB radio offi-cer replaced by a colonel. Skeletal. Avoids his doctor. Avoids his lung cancer. Smokes. Coughs. Fifties going on off-the-cliff. Known to this station only as Pinwheel. He listens.

"Kalaydoskop, Kalaydoskop. Cat's Eye to Kalay-doskop..."

He lights up and smokes.

👑👑👑

ANOTHER MANSION shares the semi-private lane that leads to Foxtail Farm. Built by a mad rail baron in the early 1800s named Paul-Pierre Gallagher who'd spent the better part of his life graphing genealogy. Be-lieved himself a descendent of Christ's second cousin. The house never updated beyond casual repair. The ge-nealogical library hidden inside the walls and in the space between two floors. Empty since the last Gallagher heir died in 2000. A classic American enchanted castle, it looms black and forbidding this Independence Day night; the only color found beyond its walls: the un-tended orange orchard. The lush fruit glows. Beautiful and strange. Impossibly orange; tempting in the silver bath of moonlight. Were the dirt and rust washed from the gatepost plaque, the manor's name would reveal itself—Garde-Joyeuse.

The pair of British Secret Intelligence Service case officers inside the dark house had not done this. Left the plaque dirty. Care would have revealed occupancy. Occupancy—their ten-week concealment inside. Clive Lancer and his MI6 supervisor, a large Scotsman called Fergus (although not his name), two decades older and more experienced than his subordinate, packed equipment. Preparatory for dawn departure. Their remaining active laptop emitted a series of chimes. The two spies shared a quizzical look.

Clive put his headset over his ears. Listened in.

"Kalaydoskop, Kalaydoskop. Cat's Eye to Kalaydoskop..."

Repeated.

Repeated.

Repeated.

The MI6 officers swiftly unpack gear. Fast hands. Fast wires. Slow software. Slow to boot. Complicated sign-in protocol. Eye authentication. Fingers clatter keys.

♕ ♕ ♕

PINWHEEL'S COMPUTER displayed Silas Kingston's dossier. A hustled-up file folder lands at his elbow. Thirty years hard copy. Corresponds/backstops. Pinwheel finishes his cigarette. Adjusts his ashtray. Positions his lighter.

"Kalaydoskop, Kalaydoskop. Cat's Eye to Kalaydoskop..."

Pinwheel answers. "Go ahead, Cat's Eye."

"Veronica-seven, Boxwood-four-ruby."

♕ ♕ ♕

FERGUS LISTENED in over a second pair of cans as Clive's hand moved his pen, rapidly filling in a security report. He transcribed Pinwheel's response: *"Switching to secure... Proceed."*

The line went static as they lost the signal, but a toothy grin drew a tea-stained line between the bush of Fergus's mustache and his summer-grown, bristly beard. "That was Mother Russia, my boy."

♕ ♕ ♕

"GET ME KALAYDOSKOP," came Silas's voice as Pinwheel studied a Soviet-era photo: Silas brush-passing a Minox film cartridge to the handsome KGB spymaster, *Kalaydoskop.*

"The Soviet Union you once served no longer exists. Kalaydoskop retired. *You* retired."

"Retirement's off; CIA Kaleidoscope is turning again. That means your Kalaydoskop turns too."

♕ ♕ ♕

SILAS'S EYES GLEAMED. He rested the mike against his lips. He spoke again. "Tell him I want in. Tell him, same rules as before."

"Your enthusiasm is appreciated, but what could you offer us now?"

"That's for Kalaydoskop only."

"And if he doesn't care?"

Silas grinned. The start of the game always a treat. "Kalaydoskop has twenty-four hours to contact me. By hour twenty-five, I will be inside FBI headquarters, confessing the truth and proving it. That for thirty years I was Russia's mole inside the CIA."

4.

MELODY SAT BACK FROM the fireworks pit. A chair alone. Contemplated her conversation with Gwen. Didn't notice Leigh behind her until the girl's arms draped around her shoulders.

"Aunt Melody?"

Melody stroked her warm skin. Peered back. *Mmm'd* an encouraging question mark.

"Is the foxtail in the name of the house a plant or an animal part?"

"Well, Papa told me when *I* asked," and here she put on a most convincing Silas impression: "'Foxtail' spelled as a compound word is the name of a marsh plant, genus *Alopecurus*, but for as long as *I've* lived here—' and you know Papa was born here, don't you?"

"Papa was born in a house?"

"This house. You know it. Aunt Linny too. And your Uncle Hal."

"What about Daddy?"

"Michael was born in Russia. Anyway, Papa said, 'For as long as I remember, every time I come home and I see the name on our gate the first American Kingstons gave this land, I can't help but picture a fox jumping into his den.'"

Silas, striding from the North Vista Outhouse carrying a heavy box, having heard this last part, took over. "And a fox's tail you never grab if his front half's down a hole!"

Melody laughed.

Leigh giggled.

For the faintest instant, Silas saw in his granddaughter not Michael but Lynn. The Lynn he'd never allowed his daughter to become. He killed the illusion. Better than killing the child inside her. Walked on. Passed Hal jogging from the pit.

"Leigh, we're about to start with the big ones. Papa's taking over. He might let you light a match or two."

Leigh's eyes widened; like all children, great excitement lived in the playing-with of matches and fire. Leigh bolted for the pit.

Melody gazed at her husband. "I'm worried about Gwen. She's so bitter tonight. About the family."

"They've had it hard even before Michael. Before all this."

"You don't think they'll split?"

"No amount of lawyers or tears can change the fact: once a Kingston, you're Kingston forever."

Melody squeezed his hand. "She has so much to be thankful for." And Melody did as well.

"She has Michael. And Michael loves her. And Silas loves Michael."

"Silas loves *all* of you."

"Even Lynn?"

Melody shook her head affectionately. "You don't get it."

👑👑👑

"YOU'LL NEVER GUESS what I found in my wine cellar this morning." Silas opened the box on the edge of the firing pit. Inside, nested in a blanket: a light infantry mortar and six illumination bombs shone Army green and dull.

While the Roman candles were reckless, this was military firepower and uncommonly dangerous. But these were Kingstons. Reared to be, in all things, above the common. Hal barely registered the relic beyond a casual, "You still have that old thing?" He jumped back into the trench.

"Couldn't exactly leave it out for Goodwill."

👑👑👑

BUZZED AND SULLEN, Gwen remained at the picnic table, watching the rest of the Kingstons.

"Mrs. Kingston?"

She turned to the sound of her name. Half-smirked at the sound of it in an English accent. Clive Lancer, looking for all the world like the college boy Paige had mistaken him for, came over. Gave her a bottle of red wine, which she accepted with a throaty "Hello, *you.*"

"I'm a friend of Paige's...?"

"You're no 'Dweeb.' Tell me the accent's a put-on... or don't."

He's gotta be fifteen years younger than me... Grrr.

"Paige and I met at the fireworks store today—Clive Lancer. She invited me."

"Who wouldn't? She's at the pit." She gestured, undressing him with her eyes as he headed off in that direction.

♕♕♕

"WATCH CAREFULLY, Paige. Papa'll tell you this is something every teenage girl should learn."

"Merlyn said, 'The best thing for being sad is to learn something.'" Paige quoted the White book back to Uncle Hal.

Hal took an illumination bomb from Silas. Hal readied it to fire.

Silas: "Cover your ears, Paige."

As she placed her hands over her ears, Paige saw Clive arrive at the dark edge of their family circle. He gave her a look that pleaded, *Don't blow my cover.*

"Firing!" Hal cried.

Karump! A puff of smoke. The bomb launched into starry skies.

♕♕♕

GURNEY-STRAPPED, hooked to life support, Lynn stared upward, the sky spinning above her. Stars sparkling, turning, falling like bits of glass inside a kaleidoscope. She fought to hold on to life as she was rushed into Emergency at George Washington University Hospital.

Seven years old, Lynn delights herself aiming a toy kaleidoscope at a mirror over the Foxtail Farm common room fireplace. She twists the end. Watches her own

*reflection break and scatter in dozens of colliding frag-
ments.*

Nurses take over from paramedics. Fight to save
Lynn's life.

*"Linny, where did that come from?" Silas glowers
from the doorway.*

"The park. A balloon man. With mommy."

Plasma—switched out. Fresh blood.

*Fresh blood paints a path along the edge of the bag-
gage carousel. The carousel circles around and back
inside. An outstretched, lifeless hand wears Michael
Kingston's wedding ring.*

*The sleeve of the jacket Lynn gave her brother at
Christmas.*

*The murdered man's face. It resembles Michael's, but
it is not him.*

♛ ♛ ♛

DAWN CAME PINK to the Limmat River in Zürich, Switzer-
land. Obscured in shadows. In gray among the trees
inside the Rentenweise Arboretum, body abused, spirit tired but undimmed, Michael Kingston stood: A spy
without order. Without commission. Without license.
Adrift of any law. A disruptor in the shadows. He lifted
what looked like a black kaleidoscope to his eye. He
tracked the passage of a 20-foot, six-door Audi lim-
ousine along General-Guisan Quai. The vehicle pulled
to courtyard gates centered in the outer wall of a staid
old building. Michael scanned the facade. Three stories.

Stacked Arzo marble. Turret office on one corner. Recognized from Cevik's photographs.

Visible in the car court, a liveried security man climbed from the front passenger side of the gray and luxurious vehicle. He walked to the rear. Opened the last door. A silver-haired gentleman disembarked. Moved with regal grace for wide and waiting glass doors. Michael clicked a button. He captured the silver-haired gentleman's image as the man mounted the steps before disappearing inside the stone building.

Michael backed deeper into the fading shadows. Michael leaned against a tree. Michael switched his monocular for his smartphone. Silver-Hair's image filled Michael's phone display. A biometric program girded the face. The program locked a match. The image identified: "Erich Antonio Abbatantuono – President/CEO, Pell & Glatisant Trading Conglomerate, GmbH."

♛ ♛ ♛

INSIDE THE BASEMENT of the Turkish Interrogation Center, the ogre, Colonel Vural, gifted Michael's gunmetal Parker ballpoint to his subordinate. He showed his back to the other man who was with them. He meticulously aligned the metal chair in front of the wall to no purpose as the two plainclothes men didn't wait for him to sit. They fired their pistols into his back. He collapsed. Knocked over the chair. Flopped onto his spine. He glared at his executioners—one he had trained and trusted, the other he had never seen before. They unloaded their remaining lead into his chest and into his head.

👑 👑 👑

THE MORTAR-FIRED ILLUMINATION BOMB rides a foxtail of sparks into the sky and explodes with more fury than all the fireworks launched that night along both shores of the Patuxent River.

The night burns white as day. The white phosphorus light—so bold, so strong—creeps over the porch rail. Creeps through the screen door with the creaky hinge. The interior French doors. Creeps into the main manor house of the Kingston family where living is forbidden. A light so powerful, it illuminates all the mirrors. All at once. Upstairs. Downstairs. It fills each one—

And perhaps this is due to Silas's careful angles in hanging them?

(Perhaps not)

—revealing the one Kingston left unaccounted.

(The still heart of the family.)

Across every wall in reflection, the light flares as the illumination round descends. In this light, Doris Kingston is seen, impossibly framed in each looking glass inside the vast plantation house. She is not like a ghost alive. Instead, she hangs by her neck from a hastily knotted rope. Flames consume her with horrid, flashing/laughing/lapping tongues of fire. For a moment, her burning corpse spins.

The effect of its duplication across the hundred and more mirrors that scale the walls is nothing so much as the view inside her daughter's long-ago childhood toy.

♕ ♕ ♕

OUT BY THE FIREWORKS PIT, beside the light infantry mortar, smoke trailing from its tube, Silas spoke: "And King Arthur said, 'Don't ever let them teach you to think; it is the curse of the world.'" Silas finished the quote from his long-dead wife's treasured book, but his hands had moved over Paige's ears, her hearing protected. Prevented. Only after he finished speaking did he remove them.

His eyes lifted to the new and strange young man who joined their company. To visit his granddaughter. Greeting her; introducing himself to the rest of them. British—a Caribbean islander, by the accent—this intruder represented all things they fired this night against.

Moscow Rules. Broken Rules.
British Embassy. Cars in/staff lockdown.
Signals out/signals unanswered.
Lights blaze. Codes fire. Cables burn.
Cold goes hot. Goes bloody.
A baby cries.
Kaleidoscope turns.
And the traitor aches at the marvel of his downfall.
For Silas Kingston, Clive Lancer held much curiosity.

About the author

Award-winning novelist Michael Frost Beckner began a Hollywood career as writing assistant to Academy Award winner Barry Levinson on "Good Morning, Vietnam" and "Rain Man". In 1989, Beckner's script for "Sniper" launched a military-thriller franchise now on its tenth sequel. Three consecutive record-breaking spec script sales and three films later, Tony Scott directed Beckner's original screenplay "Spy Game." An international hit that paired Robert Redford and Brad Pitt as CIA partners and rivals, it is now a classic in the espionage genre.

The pilot for Beckner's CIA-based television drama "The Agency" for CBS, predicted Osama bin Laden's terror attack and the War on Terror four months before 9/11. In that series alone, Beckner would go on to predict three more international terror events.

Having penned close to 100 original screenplays, adaptations, and teleplays in the employ of every major film studio, television network, and cable outlet, he is a Hollywood institution.

As a commentator on American espionage, Beckner has appeared on CNN, Fox News, CBS News, TF1 in France, and as a featured guest of Bill Maher on HBO.

Read an excerpt from:

DROUGHT

A Spy Game Novel

The Muir Trilogy Book I

By Michael Frost Beckner

Available from Montrose Station Press

October 2024

DROUGHT

To Sandy

By way of apology.

Nathan

Prologue

The Mojave

05 October 1991

1.

G OUTS OF BILIOUS GREEN fluid splattered the moth-smeared windshield—neon bright contrast to the bluish insect guts—as the Mustang gave its last: a convulsive discharge on a shower of steam. The moths. That's what did her in. A choking swarm of three-, five-, six-inch Sphinx moths in a mad, moonlit vortex some miles back. Eastern edge of Death Valley. Two freakish minutes. Like catching rounds running hazard through a crossfire of high velocity, balled-up socks. Pushed through it. Dropped down State Route 127. Turned west onto the flat, empty blacktop of the Mojave Freeway to Los Angeles. Where the needle jumped. The steam wisped. Where Nevada dawn rose on orange-rimmed, false-flamed clouds—rear-viewed behind me—to overtake my dying car. The desert highway. To overtake this fleeting night and reveal California a gray barren that dared rather than invited me forward.

Steam billowed. Radiator popped.

Twenty-five miles west of the World's Tallest Thermometer.

Twenty-five hundred miles west from Langley, Virginia.

Two days running from CIA—the Mustang, me in a bucket-seat saddle escaping the successful conclusion of Nathan Muir's Operation DINNER OUT.

One hundred miles from China Lake. Where, were I to pin it first down, all this began. Over beer, over Fritos, over cigarettes in what seems a hundred years in the past. Danny Aiken and Nathan Muir. Ol' Danny Boy. Over a question of Providence; over a question about warfare. An answer to guide my dimmed and fallen star. A chance to bring it bright again. Make my place in heaven right for when I get there. If I can get there—which is why I do what I do.

The two-spoked steering wheel thrashed in my hands as the Mustang lurched into its death throes. I wrenched the shifter to neutral. Tightened my grip. I coasted the sputtering, heat-popping, dead old Ford, crunching onto roadside gravel.

Kenyi did warn me. *"Full disclosure? You never make LA. I'd say: fuck you'n'me both, Nathan."* Pink slips traded. *"Best this old whip gives you is Col'rado. Even then you be counting yourself lucky."*

Lucky miles. Lucky since the Rockies. All bonus time since Quinter, Kansas, and a whole other Muir-engineered escape from a whole other life. *That* star.

Not this escape. Not me waiting here beside the Mustang, perched buzzard-like on a boulder—size-and-shape of a coffin—and though a man could, most days, die just sitting there, I knew *this* morning that the perfect stooge would be along soon to save me. Provide the final illusion to the Nathan Muir disappearing act.

Thanks to this Mustang dead in a puddle of engine coolant. Here.

Thanks to Kenyi, my erstwhile partner in crime. Maryland.

Thanks to China Lake—a'hundred years, a'hundred miles thataway.

I'd sensed, even though Kenyi's car was a certifiable POS, he'd had a great deal of affection for the old nag. Troubled him to part with it. His family'd had the vehicle new from the dealership. Christmas sixty-eight. "Mama's 'Stang," he'd introduced it. Mama'd loved it, too—too hard and too fast; hadn't "spared the horsewhip," he chuckled—and when Daddy took it away from her, putting her into a Pinto woody wagon, the old man gave the Mustang its first overhaul. Nights after work. Out in the garage. Some beer and radio sports. Be Kenyi's sisters' ride after that.

Daddy passed it on to the first of them in 1975. Hand-me-downed to each of the girls—"all four en'total"—as they grew up and resettled away from the blighted Jackson Ward neighborhood of Richmond, Virginia, where Kenyi's line had once been proud and prominent citizens to match their once-shining city. Still proud with most of them now escaped.

The first girl to Texas Southern in Houston; the next: University of Michigan at Ann Arbor; Kenyi's third sister—trade school-trained senior secretary—galloped all the way to 3M in Minneapolis. And each drove the other out. A little farther away each time. Each time, a pink slip ritual between them.

Each-time-after, the next youngest took the reins for the trip home. "I's the baby"—Kenyi—at fifteen, delivered his youngest sister to Portland, then returned Mama's 'Stang back into daddy's garage for a new transmission and an ass-whipping to go-along-with for driving cross country without permit or permission.

Kenyi didn't care. Came away from that with high school bragging rights until—sucked into ghetto thug life because there was nothing shining about Jackson Ward anymore—he dropped out of school. Rose to OG prominence when crack cocaine came to Richmond in 1987.

Oh, the tangled web our Agency weaves... And I won't lie and say ol' Danny and Nathan weren't witting participants on the periphery—though the "crack" aspect was the 'bangers own snap, crackle, pop twist on it with the baking soda milk.

Kenyi was a keen thinker. Kenyi cooked. Kenyi sold. Didn't smoke. Kenyi knew enough to get in, grab all, get out.

I'd discovered him some years after all those car window cash-pass, look-out, runner, corner crew, shoot-shoot, bang-bang days of yore. After he'd moved solo into the smooth glide luxury vehicle trade. He'd blipped onto the Nathan Muir radar when a Bahraini diplomat/CIA Person Of Interest had the added misfortune of getting his Mercedes Kenyi-boosted, Kenyi-chopped, Kenyi sold off in pieces—including the tracking device I'd planted for Nathan for reasons that never blew up in the Bahraini POI's, Agency, or innocent bystander faces. Parts off to parts unknown.

Mama's 'Stang. A 1969 Mustang Coupe. Touted as a "luxury" model. An under-powered rig with a remarkably hideous vinyl top which stuck out like a Red Skelton rug on the absurd comic's head, and it was anything but luxurious when Kenyi rolled it into a corner of his warehouse chop shop. Under a paint-crusted Army canvas shelter-half, it collected dust for years until I appeared in Kenyi's life and drove it away—less luxurious than that.

I convinced him I wanted it. Although it hardly worked, that old Ford would work hard enough for the kind of strange, solid-clean, highly untraceable (but-not-perfectly-so) history I needed, and—'cause what honest thief doesn't like the idea of poking a sharp stick in the shadow government's eye—? Kenyi approved my plan for the Mustang's last ride.

"Righteous end for Mama's 'Stang. Always were the family getaway car."

Getaway car for Nathan Muir, late of Langley. Headed for the coast. Early/unobserved. (Hope-against-hope.) To a place where an old spy could turn around. Back to the sea. Chamber a round. Wait for the shadow riders the shadow side of government might throw at him in pursuit.

Didn't divulge any of that last part to Kenyi—even after money and value brought us close.

His shop and the Mustang: an improvisational twist added to the "Nathan Muir Escape Hatch." A plan already in motion once Tom Bishop's capture and DINNER OUT rescue complicated an already difficult retirement day for the Cold War spy. Nathan never did get that stripper jumping out of a big ol' cake but I got a Micky-D's egg and Canadian bacon sandwich and a vanilla shake, shared from the bag Kenyi afterward slipped me my cash variance. Not at all bad, seeing his first inclination upon meeting me was to pop a cap in my skull.

"Look a'you, Milky. Standing there holdin' up my house with your shoulders all non-jalant." Kenyi bounced down from his Escalade into the night outside his open gate. "You some mutha-fuckin' lost school teacha?"

I grunted a half-grin; after all, I *was* wearing Nathan Muir elbow-patch tweed, blue button down, wide-wale corduroys and—but for my brown, gray-going hair—I'm white all over. "My professor disguise. Real me's something else entirely."

He didn't step any closer. Cocked his head. Braids spilled from a Gucci leather bucket-hat. Eyed me through gold Cartier Bulbina wood frame sunglasses darkening his view of the midnight hour we both inhabited. Made sure I got a good look at the butt of his Glock jutting from his alligator belt. A Ferragamo driving-moccasins tough guy.

Leaned up against the industrial roll-down door to his warehouse shop, I, of course, liked the man immediately. He didn't know me; never'd met me. But fully illuminated under his security lights, my hands visible, occupied with the lighting of my Panther cigarillo, and having not molested his homies chopping G-rides inside, the mood I offered Kenyi was relaxed. Was friendly. Was, I might even say, with the high beam of my half-cocked smile, something just like nonchalant.

"I know you's not a cop. An' this whole set-up—the wink an' wave you flashed my cameras: too dumb to be stupid. Dumb's gov'mint. You gov'mint?"

"Not the enforcement part."

"That the dumb part—you're way a'thinkin'?"

"Brother, it's all dumb."

"Hmm." A thumb over his shoulder. "Your 911? What's-it, a sixty-eight?"

"It is a sixty-eight," I agreed. I split the difference. "A 912. But you got the year. Few do."

Kenyi pointed a manicured finger at his waistband gun. "Why'n't I jack you right now, cockstain?"

"Because I've already brought it to you...which means there's a catch my dead body would complicate."

He wanted to grin back. I could tell. If you were going to like me, you usually did by now. But Kenyi rubbed his grin right off when he pushed his shades, two-handed, tight against his face. Peekaboo: the puzzle of a sixty-thousand-dollar green Porsche delivered to his doorstep, me chilling against that, suggested a game I was volunteering to walk him right into the winner's circle.

"Not a cop. Pre-tend professor. Gover'mint but *not* enforcement. *But* dumb. Spook? 'Cause I traded rock. Know the kinda golden 'cuffs you shadow folk offer niggas like me."

"Couldn't agree more. If I was your lawyer—"

"Ardy got me a lawyer. Got me a temper too and it's startin' to elevate."

Pushed my shoulders off his garage. Went closer. "Got me a kid who's a lawyer." My left hand held my lighter. I poked my cigarillo between my lips with my right and pointed down: my right side, herringbone pocket.

"Not int'rested in yo' boy's picture."

"We both want to keep the ignition in its original condition. Interested in my key?"

I reached. He didn't do anything with his pistol. I said, "Ditched those cuffs you mention, myself. Little before noon today. Which brings me to tonight—offering you a big old payday for a tiny bit a'work that your lawyer, mine, and any other in this land of the free would deem legal."

I dangled the Porsche's key.

"Why's it all a'whatchya sayin' make it seem the shadow folk ain't just letting you walk?"

"Well— you do have me there," I chuckled. "Sorta put the light on 'em on my way out. Gave 'em a burn."

"Like a touch-the-stove burn?"

"Like a flamethrower. Right on their cute button noses," I said and tapped the tip of mine as I snagged my smoke back from my lips.

This time, Kenyi didn't hide his grin. Aw, he did like me. Like I sort of said: when I want them to, people do. Gifted that way.

"Y'all's in a hurry, I 'magine. I ca'sell that car to someone I got in Japan. Five minutes and both of us rich when the bank's open. Seventy-thirty split...?"

I waited. Didn't need to spell it out.

Now *he* chuckled. "Same reason you think I can't jack you. Burns a'that nature leave wounds that don't heal."

I told him, "They don't want you. Won't when they find you—which, I won't lie to you 'cause we're getting on so well—they will."

He frowned.

"Not *too* soon," I soothed. "But some point down the line, be damn sure of it and be ready to talk. All part of you getting legal title to my Porsche. They won't give a shit about your work. But I'm serious, I'll need you to let 'em know what we did here." I swung my key like a hypnotist's watch. "Be cagey but cooperate. You'll tell them exactly everything that goes on between us. String it out, though and make 'em pay. They'll have no problem cashing you out for the info—they like to buy people. Two, three G's if you work 'em right."

"Then wha'-the-fuckin' point?"

"Ever throw a ball for a dog?"

He snatched the key. Couldn't resist. "So what?"

"You throw it farther and farther. Each time. Faster they bring it back, the faster and farther you throw the next ones. Further head start the dog takes on your wind up. That last one: you give it your all. Send that puppy running..."

"But you don't throw the motha'fuckin' ball."

"You do not throw the motherfucking ball. You leave them out in the middle of nowhere lost and holding their dicks."

"Am I your last throw?"

"No. I'll need a legal, dumb-but-not-stupid, untraceable car for that." I nodded to the Porsche. "Give her a tear around the block once or twice before your crew takes over."

"We gonna chop this?"

"Down to the last cap on the last air valve of the last tire."

As I watched him walk into the darkness where the Porsche waited its last ride, I heard Kenyi mutter, "Seems like murder, whip like this."

I CLAIMED THE MUSTANG, my part of the trade. Mama's 'Stang: that faded, puke-green pony with the Skelton red toupee vinyl top, on its last hoof, no one would look at twice. Never an accident. Never a moving violation. Never a shop visit thanks to Daddy; clean registration, current all the way back to '69. I took the original Ford ignition key on a quaint, black leather flap Ford dealers used to give you, the one with Phillip Clark's boldly galloping, wild horse medallion, and five-and-half grand in that fast food sack our breakfast had come in. Signed the pink slip *Nathan Muir* as damp morning oozed through the skylights and Kenyi's crew completed butchering all 90 horses of the 1968 green 912 Coupe bought direct from the AG Porsche factory in Stuttgart by an earlier Nathan Muir—the "Cold War Cowboy Muir"—just back from hauling Tom Bishop out of Indian Country and the hit his boy put on Laotian General Malo Sayasone.

EMERALD CITY.

Final sanction of EMERALD FOREST—ostensibly part of all that Golden Triangle heroin smuggle-juggle we were hooked into, but really a push-through that Nathan Muir managed for Danny Boy Aiken.

For Danny's parallel Laotian wife, Savahn.

For daughter Lara, then yet unborn. Yet uncherished.

Vixay. (He of the bright green eyes.

The green glass marbles.

Of the love [,] of the horror.)

For son Rusty: Muir-designated future Master of the game.

A CIA Cold War cowboy/dinosaur. A Johnny come lately out-of-work spy out of time— If he lets them hunt him down and snatch the last bang-bang/night-night of it from him.

And me: riding that Mustang to its bellowed death in the sunrise desert a'hundred everythings from a China Lake promise by Nathan Muir that for every innocent life I'd been party to its taking, I'd have pass on a guilty or two to balance out souls.

On the roadside. Perched on the stone coffin thrown from some prehistoric volcano. Cooking inside my skin as God turned up the Death Valley burners and the heat rolled across this wasted plain two mornings over the prairie and out of the mountains. Bonus miles. Borrowed time. His, mine, ours. I awaited the return of the tow truck I'd seen rolling in the opposite direction ten-or-so minutes before the Mustang blew its stack. Most likely a daily buzzard run, this stretch of the I-15, up to the state line and back.

Radiators, Alternators, Batteries, Tires: faded blue in cursive along its white Century Wrecker flanks. That was two hours ago. Before even the first engine knock or wisp of steam. The tow truck driver wasn't looking for me then; he'd find me soon enough.

Those who *were* looking? The last sighting anyone had of Nathan Muir—any of them who mattered—would be Silas Kingston, Counterintelligence chief. Dulles Airport. Where he watched Nathan Muir walking to a plane to Florida retirement Nathan never caught and never wanted. And now they know. Now they would be coming.

2.

A HAIRY ARM COATED in road dust. Propped on the sandblasted white ledge of his wrecker door. "That's a classic," said the tow truck mechanic.

"If Ford's best shot at underpowered and ugly's your measure. Guess so."

He blinked. Blond, girlish lashes over stuporous eyes. Bushy eyebrows above. Dusty as his arms. "Sphincter moths done-up your radiator, *enh?* If it's justa flush, even a straight re-place—they gitcha that bad—fan belt, brakes, basic clutch-work: trus'-me to get you going in a jif'," he grinned. A hillbilly by every measure except for elevated landscape. Teeth to match "Mama's 'Stang"—color and decay. "Let's get it back to my shop n'up on the rack. We'll give her a look-see." He shook his head, all corny-like and pleased. "Them moths like flyin' tamales, I swar-t'God."

He picked one from the wipers; corn husk wings and pulpy body. Weren't wrong.

"Not much else to do with my time, sitting here otherwise," I said.

"Cook to death?" he suggested. Winked, those oddly pretty lashes tossing dust. "They call it 'Baker' for a reason." He sniggered, riffing a stupid pun off the name of the last town.

Told him he could hook up his rig and haul my dead horse to his tannery and he waited on that. Less an idea what I was saying than I'd had with his pun, and that's the cross purpose we spoke to. A cross purpose that would define us for the rest of his abbreviated life.

👑 👑 👑

A LONG RIDE into deep nowhere. We rolled into his yard. A couple mutts, rigged from spare dog parts, scattered across the crumbly asphalt driveway. Leaped a zigzag of whitewashed tractor tires that outlined the crooked approach. A large man in stained overalls played with a Tonka truck in the middle of the drive. He needed the horn to motivate him out of his dirt patch.

"Eldest boy."

'Round about thirty years of age, the "boy" with the toy truck flashed a smile like his old man's—dentally ragged, though less bullshitty. Carefree idiocy. He was missing an eye. He waved. I waved back. And he hardly noticed, or remembered two seconds later, when he shuffled to the lee of a single-wide mobile home. A forlorn woman, slowly becoming an upright lizard—pinched gray skin, unforgiving eyes, tongue-tip splitting the edges of lipless jaws—watched my arrival from her miserable worldview basking on the trailer's slapdash stoop.

Noticing my squint: "Weren't always like that. The boy that is—not my bee-atch." He laughed through his nose. Reminded me of one of those Disney animatronic jug band bears: mechanical twitches, a permanent, moonshine-y smirk, with the fat folds of his rubber neck rolling right up into his cheeks. He said, "His wife-a'left'-im—was up dealing cards at Primm. Getting a poke from her pit boss on the side. Kid grabbed his pistol— So far so good, right?"

I didn't care.

He maneuvered his rig past the shop area. Began what would be a five-point turn that didn't get my wreck aimed anywhere useful.

"'Cept he decides to shoot hisself. 'Stead a'her. Get it? Blasts his own eye out and piece a'his brain—which he didn't have much of to begin with."

We climbed down from the cab.

"That dog right there?" He indicated a big, red tongue-loller. "Et it."

"Which?"

"Whaddya mean 'which'?"

"Eye or brain?"

"Both. Never been the same since."

"The dog?"

He screwed his face at me—Like I said, "cross-purposed"—as vacant as his eldest boy's, while another son—mid-twenties, clean coveralls, shaggy hair, wolfish eyes—wandered out of the garage. Polished a socket wrench with a cloth. Stopped short like cops do. Crooks, too. Polished the tool for no apparent reason other than it's the sort of thing he must have seen mechanics do on TV. It was he, the sight of him—looking past me to his mother, a peculiar obedience, that's all you could call it—who moved the needle from weird to worse.

We stood in front of the three lift bays. Me playing dumb to the non-verbal argument I watched range loud between father, mother, sons—at least the one. The one to watch out for.

That's when I saw it. On the far rack, up high near the dirt-on-grime-on-flaps of peeling ceiling paint, hung a Mercury Sable with Oregon plates. Tags: this month current.

What'd we got—this middle of nowhere shithole? A single gas pump. From before digital. Rusted into a weed planter. Weeds long dead. The aforementioned lizard trailer. An office—a space-age Stardust Casino look: a flat, faded blue, kidney-shaped roof with square-cut glass windows below, patterned with red-brown desert dirt that resembled a blast of diarrhea in a dried-out toilet bowl.

Memory hit: a Matamoros whorehouse. Cleaned out and left bloody. All except that filthy crapper with the last dead guy's last pepper-yellow turd staring back up at me along with a piece of his jaw.

An old mechanical cash register just visible inside. On the counter, piles of crinkled triplicate work orders—white-yellow-pink—palled the dead black flies. Gathered dust. A skeletal wire rack that once held snacks. Mister Coffee—with a broken handle pot. The whole place given up without the last, vacating roach bothering to tell the humans.

And there sure wasn't anybody inside on the flaking orange Naugahyde, rust-speckled chairs, holding a Mercury keyring.

So, where's Oregon?

Behind the service station, poorly blocked from sight by a mishmash of stacked tires and barrels, corrugated iron, plastic-leaf slotted chain link, and sunburnt yellow, practically-see-thru fiberglass, spanned a two-acre graveyard. Over two hundred cars, trucks, trailers; some boats; random appliances; construction and farm machines; a few kicked in, knocked over once-navy cooked-to-sky-blue honey buckets. A monument garden to abandoned futures and discarded pasts. Mama's 'Stang would fit right in. That didn't stop me from feeling bad for it.

"I dropped my last older sister, Lashay, at George Fox University in Portland—became a trauma nurse."

"If I get out to Portland, I'll give her my regards."

"Naw. She passed."

"Sorry. Too young."

"How the muthafucka-did-it wanted her."

"Catch the guy?"

Kenyi glanced off, grim, frustrated. Mood shift. Grin. "You so full-a'shit, Nathan, this deal," Kenyi called me by my cover. Backhanded my shoulder. "Whole family loved Mama's green 'Stang. You make sure she goes out right."

We toasted fast food milkshakes. Yum.

"Where's 'Oregon'?" I asked Hillbilly Bear, jutting my chin at the Mercury.

He glanced at his son who twirled the bright-shiny socket wrench like the girl who didn't make cheerleader.

"Back order on parts," Socket answered. "Taken care of. Once UPS arrives we'll be done with that one in jiff."

"Not what I asked."

"Be in Baker. They doing just fine," half-sang Hillbilly Bear.

"'They'? 'They' a 'he'?"

If a scorpion a mile out in the desert just now sneezed, I'd have heard it in the stillness created by the lack of response.

Socket dropped his wrench into his back pocket. Finally said, "Don't see how that's your business. Mister."

My business because I make it my business. Because you are not a "local" mechanic, bub. Because someone who lives in Baker doesn't drop off their car with you; got a Baker garage for that. Because that Sable belongs only to someone who was passing through—

But didn't.

And we're all just now, like a happy family, sharing this same set of conclusions that Oregon's still somewhere and probably not where "they" should be.

And I am not family.

And that's making you unhappy and uncomfortable. Me, too.

Socket lowered the Mustang from the wrecker. "Let's get this heap inside, Pops. Take a look."

"Just naturally curious," I blustered. I pushed. "Like to know how long I'll be with you. Things to do in LA."

They tacitly ignored me.

Pushed more, blustered more. "'Oregon' get an Auto Club rate through you guys—to rent a room?"

"Like we said," Hillbilly Bear intoned, "you'll be outta here in a jiff." Proclamation intonation. His intention announced to his family—*I want him outta here.*

The mobile home hatch smacked shut. That's how much Lizzie Lizard liked that.

"We'll take a *careful* look, Pa." Socket, flat. Big veto backing mama's door slam.

"Take-a-take-a take a look." Sing-songed back from Kid Popeye, once more plopped down in his dirt patch. *Vroom-vroom*, shoving his yellow tin truck through asphalt chunks.

Socket got inside the Mustang. Steered. Hillbilly Bear shoved from the rear. Me, I watched. Mama's ol' green 'Stang rolled into the empty center stall.

Rip-off artists. All they are.

Too easy, too sweet—tap a pocket, lighten a wallet, squeeze a credit card dry, but keep your victims rolling through.

Anything else—how long's something like that last?

If they're in the game...?

Lasts forever.

"Take your time, guys." Blustered. "Oh, you *do* make a deal if I want to go straight cash for the whole thing, right?" Pushed.

A little Old Blue Eyes from my lost record collection, my lost family, my lost life:

"Someone's calling, hear him sigh..."

A father-son moment—*straight cash?* Their eyes danced one to the other.

"Grown-up records, Rusty." I told my son. "Don't touch them while I'm gone."

I gave the Mercury a longer look. "Hello, Kitty," in her little red bow, waved back at me from the rear window. If they can get a Ford out in "jiff," be the same for a Merc'. Same standard parts, or the car would already be out in the hillbilly graveyard.

The Ghost-in-the-Graveyard "Hello, Kitty." (Run, run, run!)

The plate frame: "I'd Rather Be Shopping at Nordstrom."

A woman's car. A woman stashed in Baker.

Old Blue Eyes—

"Through the black of night

I've got to go where you are

If it's dark or bright

I've got to go where you are..."

China Lake. The law of unintended consequences. The Nathan Muir business of collateral damage.

With the Mustang expired, my job playing my old boss, my best friend, my "big brother" was over. Time to make the Nathan Muir dog ball disappear. Prometheus unbound. Time to go back to being a piece of twenty-year roadkill on a sunflower-y highway outside Quinter, Kansas.

And I, a living wraith with a penance to pay, a vengeance to prevent, as long as I'm ol' Danny Boy alive: I pry another of Vixay's green marbles from the slavers' puddled footprints in the Cambodian mud and acknowledge that there are no certainties. Anywhere.

Part One

Los Angeles

05 October 1991

"Perhaps you yourself have notions about the Glass Bead Game, expecting more of it than it will give you, or perhaps the reverse. There is no doubt that the Game has its dangers. For that very reason we love it; only the weak are sent out on paths without perils."

—Herman Hesse, *The Glass Bead Game*

3.

PHILOSOPHER KARL MARX ARGUED that uncertainty and chance in social dynamics was only the *appearance of the thing* since all social actions were directed and produced by deliberate intention. Though Danny Aiken justifiably despised the communist for his global legacy of mass murder, he grudgingly agreed with the old German's theory on blowback. He used it to justify what he'd do a little later in the fly-crap, hot-time town of Baker.

Kenyi, a timely Apollo to my asset's Admetus (whom none of us could ever repay), quoted Danny's application of the theory to Hillbilly Bear—pistol kissing the fat man's ear:

"'Unintended consequences' are consequences that should be expected but never are. Obtained unconsciously, they were from the very first step you took in the path that's led us to this just end, secretly desired by all parties. Any surprise you feel right now—this exact moment— ol' Hillbilly Bear—is your slow-witted mind catching up too late to the lie you told yourself to hurry you here."

✹✹✹

DESTINY SHAKING HANDS with Fate. That's how I'd put it. And these days, that's the kind of handshake I need to avoid. Both GLADIO and Silas Kingston's KALEIDOSCOPE had plenty of reason to grab my hand and rattle me until my teeth fell out. A "howdy-do" over my life and, possibly, continued entitlement to it. Then, there's Cuban DGI; if Danny's kid Rusty and Nina Alverez don't thread the Charlie March needle down in Havana, it's going to be—well, no use prolonging the metaphor—violent. GLADIO, Silas, Cuban commies: the pissed-off-at-Nathan-Muir trifecta. All of them desire my silence. But will they seek it—part, or all? One by one or all at once? Results are the same. I end up dead. Per my instructions, Danny Aiken had thrown the Nathan Muir dog ball deep into the Mojave and, temporarily at least, removed me from unintended consequences' inconvenience.

Around the time Danny Aiken watched "Mama's 'Stang" rise on the lift beside the Mercury Sable he planned to rummage through later, I stood veiled beneath the sap-sweaty branches of a Chinese elm. In front of a San Fernando Valley three-bedroom, ranch-style house I'd once purchased to be my home. My future. My happily-ever-aftered Amen.

Yours or Tom's bad idea—paint the whole thing muddy green? Turn my back on you, Sandy, one lousy minute...

(Sometimes our most flagrant mistakes are our most precious intentional choices.)

Hell. It's six years since I've laid sight on it. More than twenty years since I've been inside. Yet, who's to say the math doesn't work out—when more than once every minute, you and Tom nurse at my thoughts?

♔♔♔

WHEN I WAS A YOUNG MAN and these ramblers were all the rage, they dubbed them Cinderella Homes. I thought that rather trite. Still do. But I was back from Cyprus and the Enosis, back from the dead drops and drop-dead pipe bombs; I was young and I was back from my first overseas assignment with Charlie March. Back in that time of youth when the prospects of a life in service as a Clandestine Officer of the Central Intelligence Agency opened ahead of me as broad and gaudy as a happy-ending backdrop luring my Bob Hope to Charlie March's Bing Crosby on a riotous road to eternal damnation. Back when I was young, and I still believed righteous execution sanctified dead-kid brain and skull spatter. When tap water and bar soap was holy enough to purify murder with a lather of my hands. Back before I understood "home" was like my deadly/dead mentor's leonine smirk the morning I fell for his recruitment. That—

"Work of the Nation,"
"Ye shall know the truth,"
"True faith and allegiance,"
Rule of Thumb bullshit—

I'd swallowed hook, line, and *match*: the match that ignited the unquenchable soul-fire that is this game that's become the be-all before the end-all of me.

Before I understood the gruesome truth that "home" wasn't a ticket awarded me, but a marker I brightly surrendered to pass through the magic theater door that only opens one direction.

After the one—

[a claim check on my life]

fucking Cyprus

but before the other—

[on my soul]

permanent dissociation

—here I am in front of the house I didn't make my *Amen* but abandoned to my wife and our baby. I strip that pea soup paint with my mind's eye and see the home new. Available. Desirable for all that it has to offer that I cannot touch. And I hear across the years—

"Why, Nathan, it's the very one in the picture!" Your white-gloved finger taps the Los Angeles Times *advertisement.*

The drawing: 1950s newlywed cake-toppers alighted from a Princess's crystal pumpkin carriage beneath a weeping willow; there's a chubby little dude in breeches, tailcoat, and curly wig beneath tricornered hat—half-coachman half-fairy godfather—half-bowed, arm bowed, urgently extending a welcome that makes my new wife gleefully exclaim—

"As I live and breathe, that might as well by our Charlie. Oh, Nathan. Let's buy this *house."*

Since I didn't know better about our brother/brother-in-law, mentor-in-smile/Charlie March/traitor, I laughed along with Sandy—Muir, née March, now Bishop (how's that for a bowl of nuts?)—and bought us this "very" California Cinderella ranch-style rambler painted in respectable, nothing-to-see here, fade-out gray.

August 7, 1952.

Same day the *Herald-Examiner* ran a photo of a gas-masked man. He's downtown LA. A cluster of gawking goofballs. He's selling balloons with the sign that reads: *FRESH CLEAN DESERT AIR – BALLOONFULL 50¢.*

When I was young and the chumps in that photograph and all my new neighbors in the Valley didn't know half of what would go into the LA atmosphere before CIA was through with us; back when housing tracts didn't come with their own freeway off-ramp; back when housing tracts didn't need dedicated zip codes to make sense of their massive indifference; back when God forgave even murder, but I never could, and I kept at it, government sanction, and I let it grow—define me—that devouring tapeworm curled and lengthening within the bowels of my life. That thing that keeps me hungry and the best at what I am/now-was as it softly nibbles my soul into nothing.

The heat hadn't been so atrocious back in '52. Then everyone in Los Angeles went ahead and dug a swimming pool. Planted a moist green lawn. Watered it twice a day. Turned the dry, sooty air of this desert-basin valley into a humidity trap.

It's eight in the morning and already the wet fevered weather (always count on a heatwave around World Series time) shimmers from the concrete sidewalk rolling hot to the neighborhood corners. From the asphalt, the stink of street tar mixes with backyard chlorine, and the tang of eucalyptus monoterpenes bleeds into the air from the groves long-ago planted—some say for the railroad, others as windbreaks for the long-gone Valley bean farms—each tree grown over one hundred feet high. Dusky giants visible over the back of Sandy's house. They edge the vacant field beyond her garden wall. Extend like ancient soldiers in line of march along the edge of Bull Creek that runs deep, natural, and wild across the Sepulveda Basin to the plunging concrete wash and the loud and poisonous Ventura Freeway two miles away.

Cineole, pinene, limonene, cymene: monoterpenes. Drought times like these, they boil into the sky.

👑👑👑

"GENTLEMEN: KENNEDY SLAPPED our balls in a vice with Operation SWITCHBACK. No doubt, Johnson's cranked the handle. But while we're stuck running half-assed covert ops under Pentagon control, at least the Army can't control Southeast Asia's weather, so we got that going for us, right?"

We made a noise that approximated the polite chuckle required by his nerdy smirk—Herb Weisshart our Deputy Chief, Combined Studies Division, Saigon Station, regaling us back in the summer swelter of '64.

"Well, I'm here to tell you: our Agency can. Turns out, it's solely and entirely in our power to make it rain wherever whenever we want. Monoterpenes—that's the final ingredient to the secret sauce, or so they tell me."

I was in Saigon from Vientiane, Laos, paving the way for Operation POPEYE. A couple case officers from out of Long Cheng. Another pair of logistics guys from Air Studies Branch OP 32 and Air Studies Group OP 75, crew cut and buttoned downed, who fronted a sextet of Air America jockeys and kickers who crewed a new batch of unmarked, unaccountable US Forest Service planes recruited/rotated in from—how's this for opposites?—Glacier National Park, Montana.

One of the pilots quipped a movie line, "'We don't believe in rainmakers.'"

His kicker—former USN, current USFS, reassigned CIA—quipped back in perfect Burt Lancaster bass, "What DO you believe in, Mister? Dyin' cattle?'" Delivered with a cockeyed grin he shot like a pistol.

He got real laughs. And me? I'd been a sucker for that crooked grin since I'd roped him in back at China Lake. The first time. His name was Daniel Aiken. As our lives intertwined, I've called him Danny Boy ever since.

"Alright. Easy now," said Weisshart.

👑👑👑

"Like vines," Danny Boy said, standing in the rain on a Kansas highway, five years later in 1969. Dead of night. He's helping me plant dead body evidence that would prove him deceased. Would set him free—as I'd made and kept to our promise—to fully embrace the green marble curse he'd chosen as his destiny. "The only way we reach the light at the top of this jungle we're still climbing out of is like we've always done: by growing and climbing off each other."

"Danny Boy, a vine's just a dumb jungle plant."

"And yet, ol' Prometheus, those dumb creepers know-exact the secret of survival."

Daniel Aiken. Whose son I would accept as my charge. A certain daughter too, whose secret I would protect, and I would nurture both as my own in (if you allow me these lies to stand for all three of us), my own inimical way...

♛ ♛ ♛

WEISSHART GESTURED one of our Agency meteorologists take over. Couple of perspiring pencil-necks flown in, agog, from Thailand. The one who spoke gave the pride of ownership explanation no one bothered to decrypt, that ended with:

"Really, it wasn't that difficult once we figured out that vegetation—releasing excessive amounts of monoterpene chemical compounds during severe drought—make an emergency bond with whatever scant water evaporation is rising into the air. It's nature's attempt to create and thicken clouds. To conversate—if I may—jungle to cloud, thereby to induce sudden heavy rain.

"By this we de-duce it isn't about bringing the cloud to earth but also elevating essential plant oils skyward to make the cry for 'help'—if you will—upward to the cloud. Come in on top, mix the passing clouds with silver and lead iodine—two of the primary sources of water condensation nuclei—seed at altitude, and convert cloud vapor into ice crystals, and we can produce or—if you will—create monsoon season year-round..."

Weisshart cut back in. "So, screw the ambush prisoner grabs. Flip the bird on the village asset who's playing both sides. And fuck the infiltrations that vanish as soon as we insert them over the line. We'll let the Pentagon hold their own asses on the intelligence gathering of dubious result. We know what makes these little zipperheads tick. Rice, rice, more rice, and a fast-moving trail to carry it hither and yon to their armies.

"What Mr. Peabody and Sherman here are telling you, is we got the know-how and now the go-how to flood their paddies, wash away their ant-trail, pin them down, and drown the NVA and their VC running dogs out of rations. Oldest effective strategy in the book: surrender through starvation."

We seeded the crap out of the skies over North Vietnam. Over Laos. Over Cambodia...

Killed a few folks with it, too—closer to L.A. than to anywhere Ho Chi Minh cut trail. And not by starvation. Floodwater just as lousy as washing that kind of dirt from the hands as a kitchen tap in a Cinderella dollhouse.

I stood at her door. I clanked the dainty knocker against the speakeasy grill announcing myself as hard as I could. Sandy didn't bother to unlatch the viewport but yanked open the door—too quickly to not have been watching—and I saw her for the first time in six years.

I presented my cheek.

Step right up: Lips? Palm? Brass knuckles?

"You make it awfully hard, Nathan."

"Hard for what?"

"To spit in your face."

I faced her. I spread my lips to show her how nicely my teeth sparkled with my cornflower eyes. "Dare you."

I've loved you, sweet Sandy. I really did.

She pinched my chin between her thumb and first knuckle. "You didn't need-come all the way out. I thought I was clear with that fool attorney of yours."

"Ah, Dumbo's alright."

She scowled, mocking me mocking Danny Boy's son. "It's been six days. I've heard from Harry Duncan in Hong Kong. I've *spoken* to Tom. He knows everything." She bit her lower lip. "He doesn't blame me..." She Barbie-dolled her emotions under a rubber grin. "But God's truth, he hates your guts."

"Hated me for years. Seems to drive us further together. Way I see it, knowing I'm his father might just get his focus back. Let him accomplish something without me."

"He said to tell you he's going to kill you."

"Yep. That attorney of mine you think's stupid told me the same. Wouldn't be something I don't deserve. I'm sure."

"Then 'welcome.'" She pulled the door wide. "Come on inside. Wait."

I didn't move. "He'll be a while. Headquarters needs to fully debrief him. Soon as possible. Everything they're putting him through right now in HK is pregame to the rough match ahead at Langley if he wants to get out of this clean."

She hesitated on a tiny gasp of hope. "Do you think they'll terminate his contract? Let him out...entirely?"

I don't like to let Sandy down, but it's a habit I'd perfected our entire lives. "They'd like to. He'd like it even more. Not going to happen. Not after I busted him out of that Chinese prison *not* on their behalf. Operationally, practically, legally, spiritually: too tangled. Neither the Agency nor Tom can afford anything other than making peace and pretending it was their big deal all along."

"Then why are you here?"

Already exhausted by me.

And my being.

And my being here.

"I need to tell you about your brother."

There was that briefest of moments. The kind that feels much longer than it takes to pass. Those couple seconds when Sandy pretended not to know exactly what she knew I meant.

Surrounded by spies.

Her Brother. Her ex-husband. Her son.

Surrounded by deceit.

Surrounded by our killing.

Hell of a life we've done her in for.

Sandy abruptly turned. She couldn't see me, but I raised my hands and reached. If she were still mine, and my touch still meant something, I'd have gently held her shoulders.

Her back to me, she said, "Want a drink?"

I lowered my hands.

"Need to be off the sauce. For now. Turns out, it's me who's been terminated," I said. "Only here because

I need some time to make sure 'terminated' isn't a euphemism."

She cupped a hand at the base of her spine. Opened it toward me. I touched her palm with the tips of my fingers.

"You still smoke though, right?"

She didn't look back.

"Mmm." I left my fingers, feeling her coolness. She let me. Didn't look back either when I dropped my bomb. "Your brother's dead."

Her fingers clamped. Hard. "Then you'll light me a cigarette and tell me you had a good reason to do it."

"Thanks heaps. Why immediately think it was me?"

And bang: she shot me wild eyes. "Because Charlie always said it would be." Eyes that communicated both her collected hate and some small portion of remembered love; communicated an untamed joy that her cage door had suddenly sprung wide, and a darker misery that it only released her into a larger prison. But in those gray eyes that combined with the blue of mine lived the eyes of our son. Lived the recognition of both the illusion of and the utter necessity for reckless abandon in the face of the unpredictable future and irrefutable past I represented. In Sandy's face was the conscious moment one chooses to laugh at the inescapableness from the map drawn at our birth that assigns us to our lives.

She tugged me off balance and inside. I kicked shut the door with my prosthetic foot and didn't feel a thing.